STAR WARS

CLONE WARS

ADVENTURES

VOLUME 2

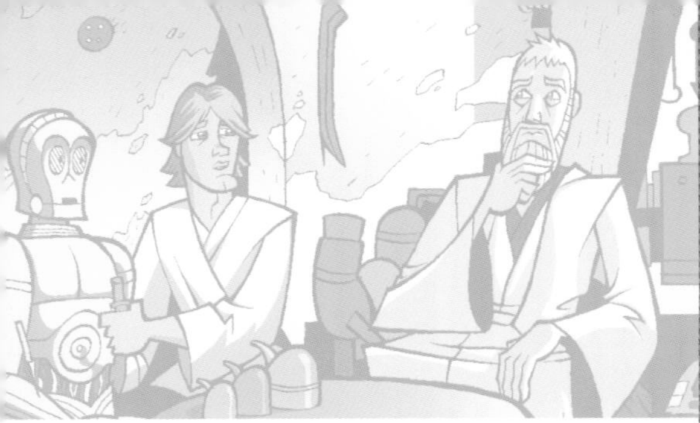

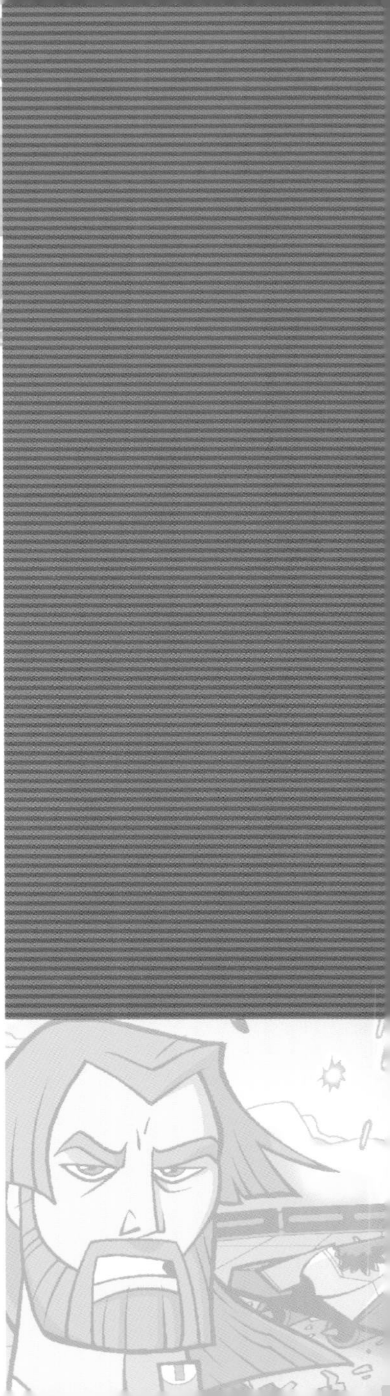

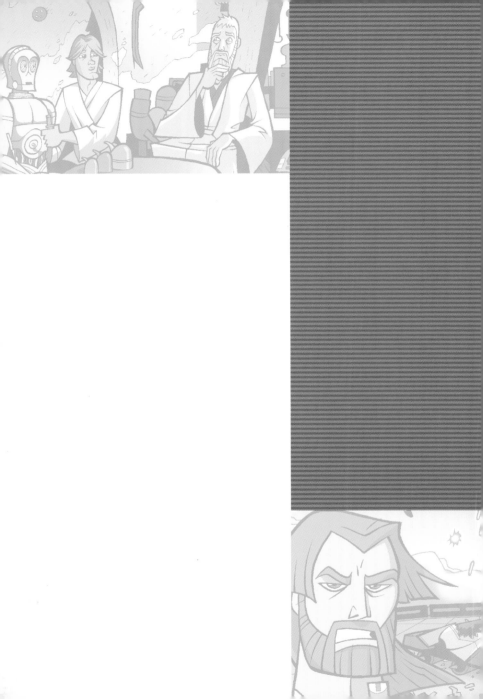

STAR WARS®

CLONE WARS
ADVENTURES
VOLUME 2

SKYWALKERS
script **Haden Blackman**
Additional dialogue by George Lucas
From *Star Wars*: Episode IV *A New Hope*

art **The Fillbach Brothers**
colors **Wil Glass**

HIDE IN PLAIN SITE
script **Welles Hartley**
art **The Fillbach Brothers**
colors **Sno Cone Studios, Ltd.**

RUN MACE RUN
script and art **The Fillbach Brothers**
colors **Wil Glass**

lettering
Michael David Thomas

cover
The Fillbach Brothers and Dan Jackson

Dark Horse Books®

visit us at www.abdopublishing.com

Reinforced library bound edition published in 2012 by Spotlight,
a division of the ABDO Group, 8000 West 78th Street, Edina, Minnesota 55439.
Spotlight produces high-quality reinforced library bound editions for schools and
libraries. Published by agreement with Dark Horse Comics, Inc., and Lucasfilm Ltd.
Printed in the United States of America, Melrose Park, Illinois.

052010
092010

 This book contains at least 10% recycled materials.

Special thanks to Sue Rostoni and Amy Gary at Lucas Licensing

Cataloging-in-Publication Data

Blackman, Haden.
Star wars: clone wars adventures. Volume 2 / script Haden Blackman ;
art the Fillbach Brothers ; colors Wil Glass and Sno Cone Studios ;
lettering Michael David Thomas ; cover art the Fillbach Brothers and Dan Jackson.
Clone wars adventures -- Reinforced library bound ed.
p. cm. -- (Star Wars: Clone wars adventures)
1. Star Wars fiction--Comic books, strips, etc. 2. Graphic novels. I. Filbach Brothers.
II. Thomas, Michael David. III. Title. IV. Title.
V. Title: Star wars, Clone wars (Television program) VI. Series.
741.5'973 --dc22

ISBN 978-1-59961-905-7 (reinforced library bound edition)

All Spotlight books are reinforced library binding
and manufactured in the United States of America.

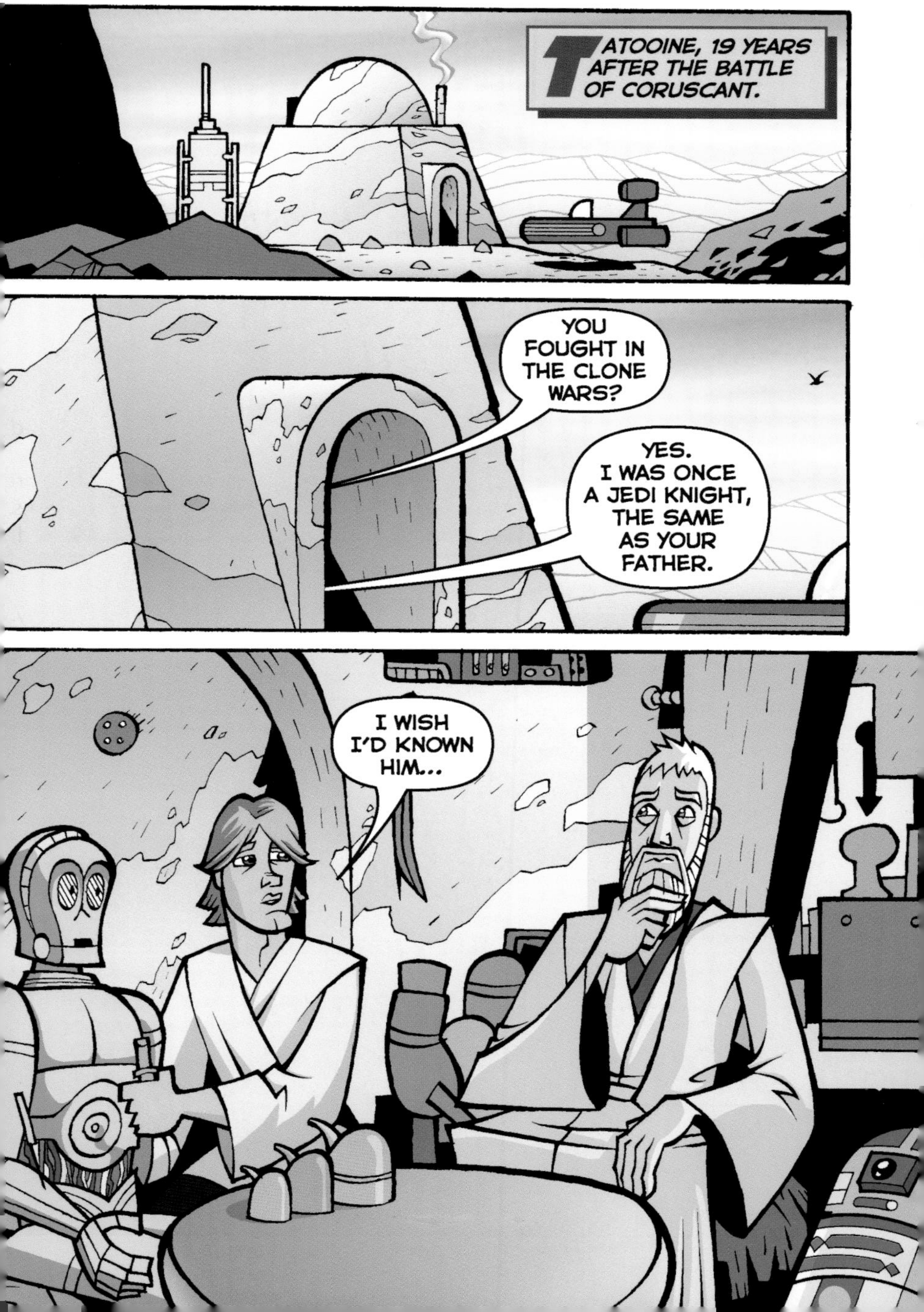
TATOOINE, 19 YEARS AFTER THE BATTLE OF CORUSCANT.
YOU FOUGHT IN THE CLONE WARS?
YES. I WAS ONCE A JEDI KNIGHT, THE SAME AS YOUR FATHER.
I WISH I'D KNOWN HIM...

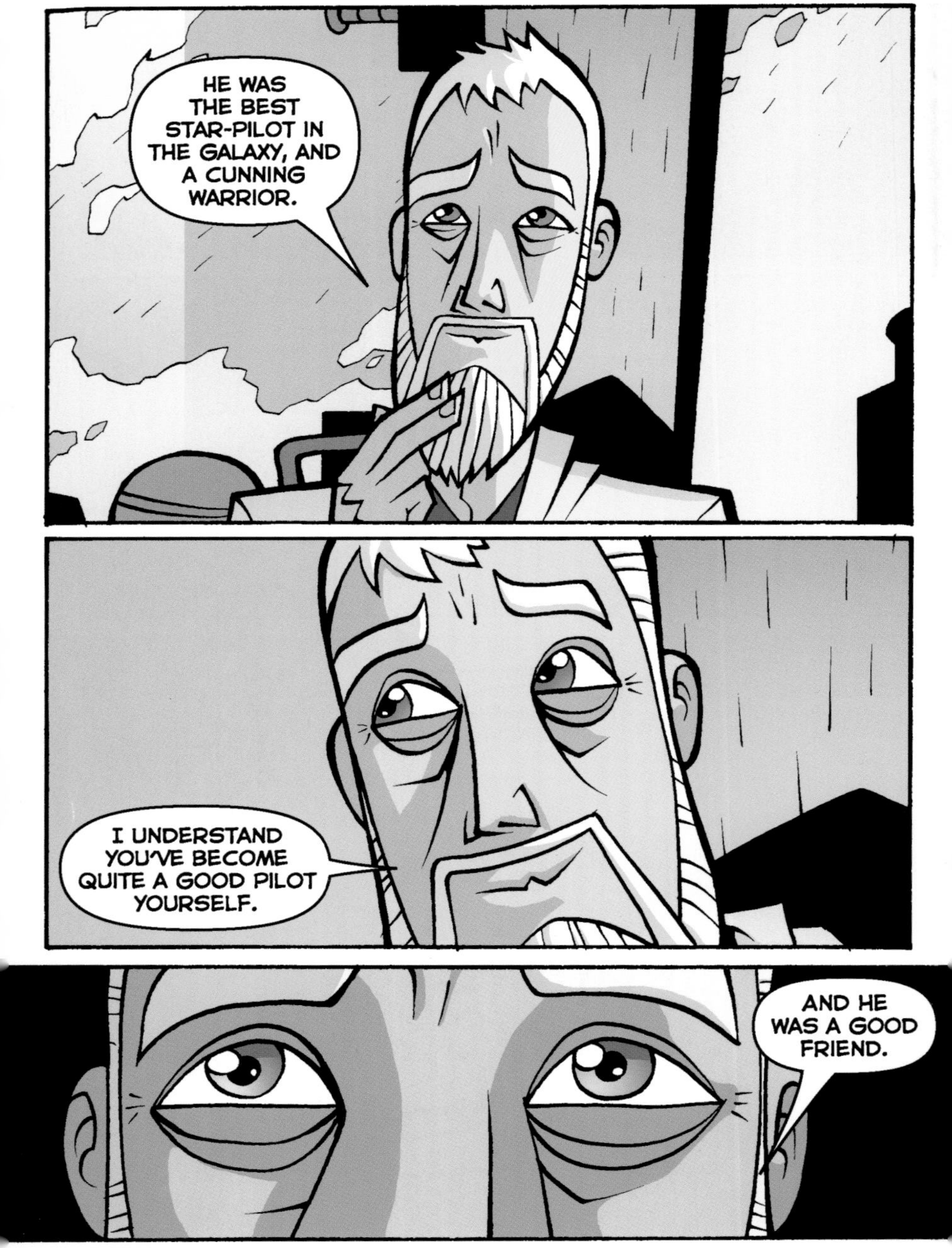
HE WAS THE BEST STAR-PILOT IN THE GALAXY, AND A CUNNING WARRIOR.
I UNDERSTAND YOU'VE BECOME QUITE A GOOD PILOT YOURSELF.
AND HE WAS A GOOD FRIEND.

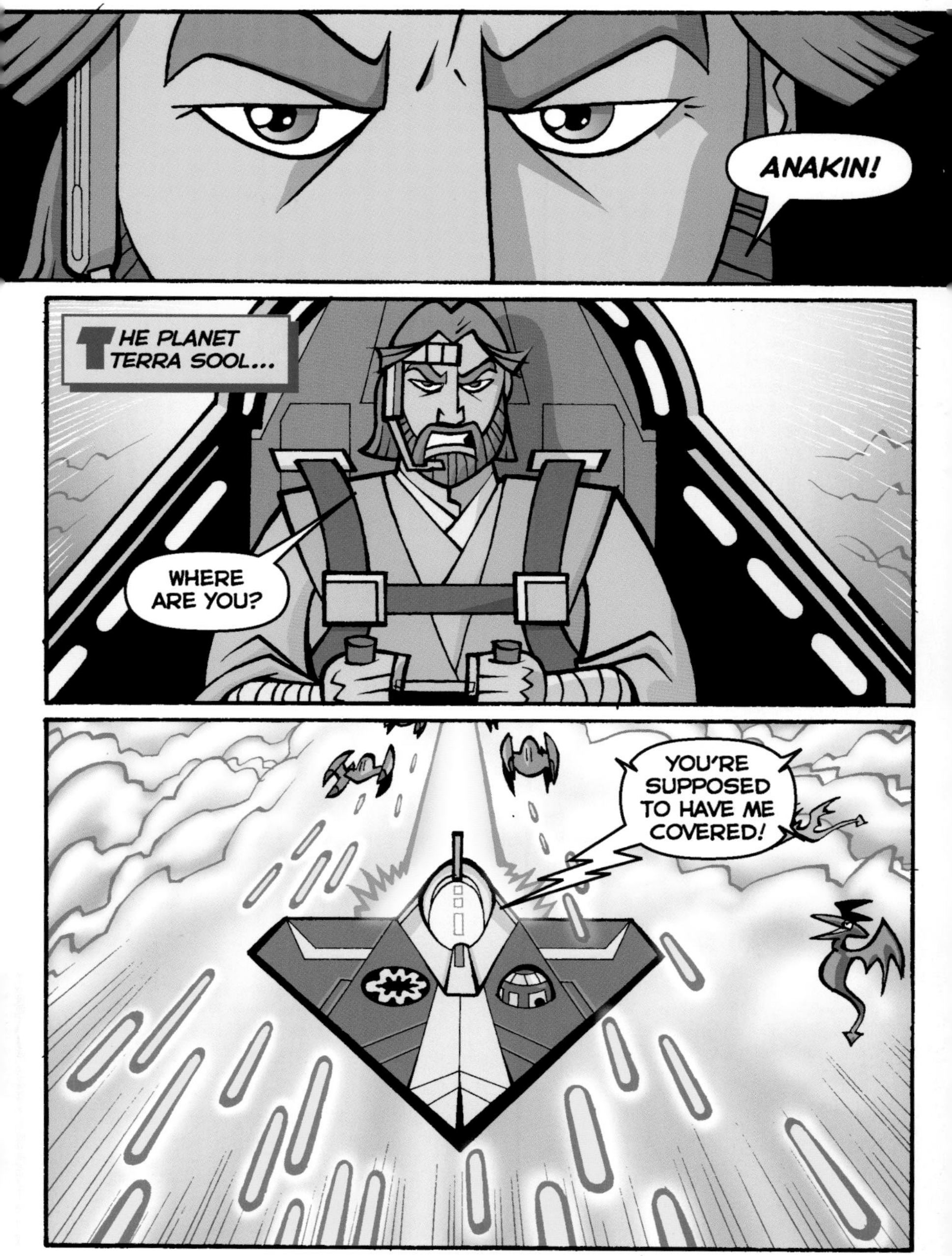
ANAKIN!
THE PLANET TERRA SOOL...
WHERE ARE YOU?
YOU'RE SUPPOSED TO HAVE ME COVERED!

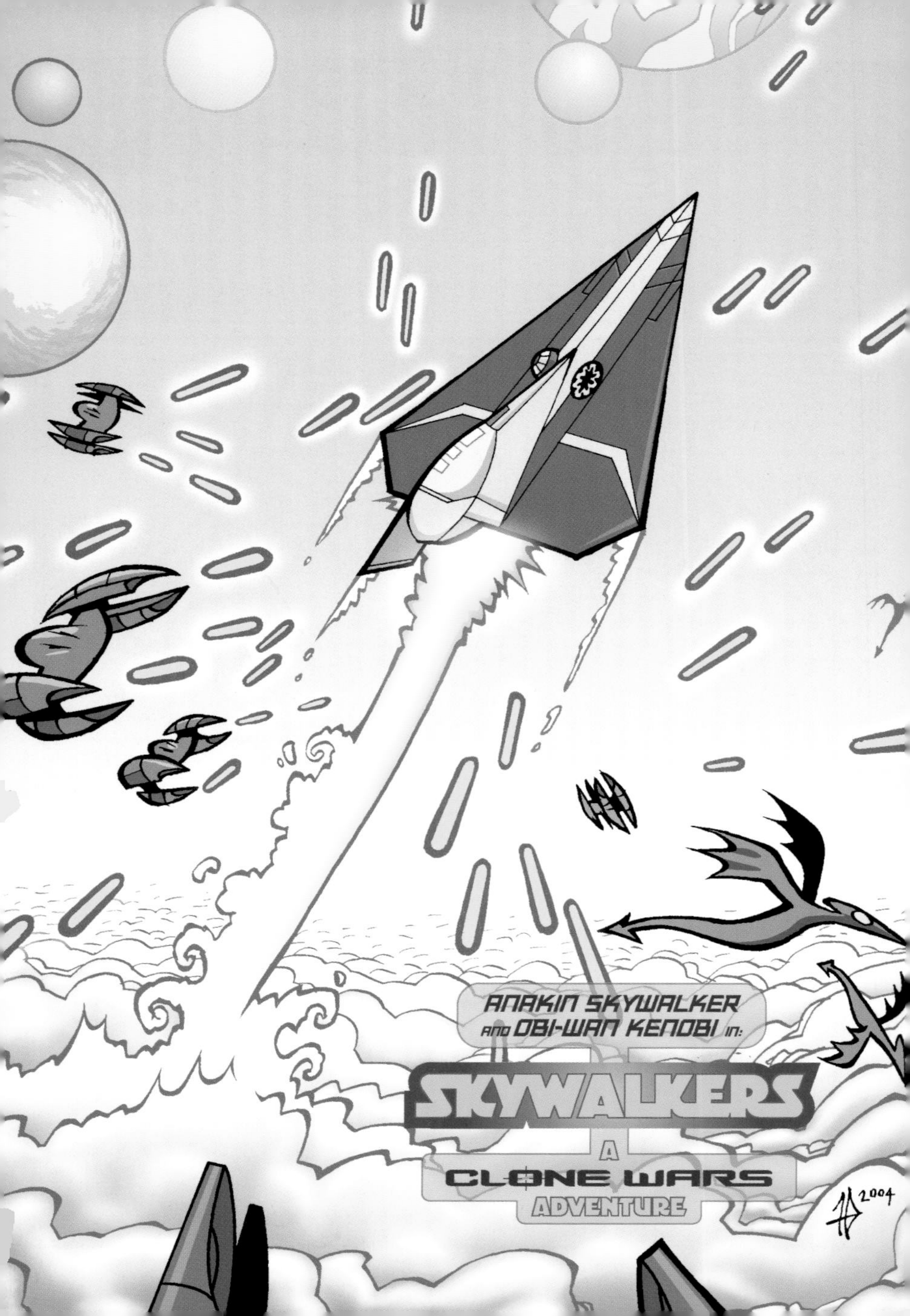
ANAKIN SKYWALKER
AND OBI-WAN KENOBI IN:
SKYWALKERS
A
CLONE WARS
ADVENTURE
2004

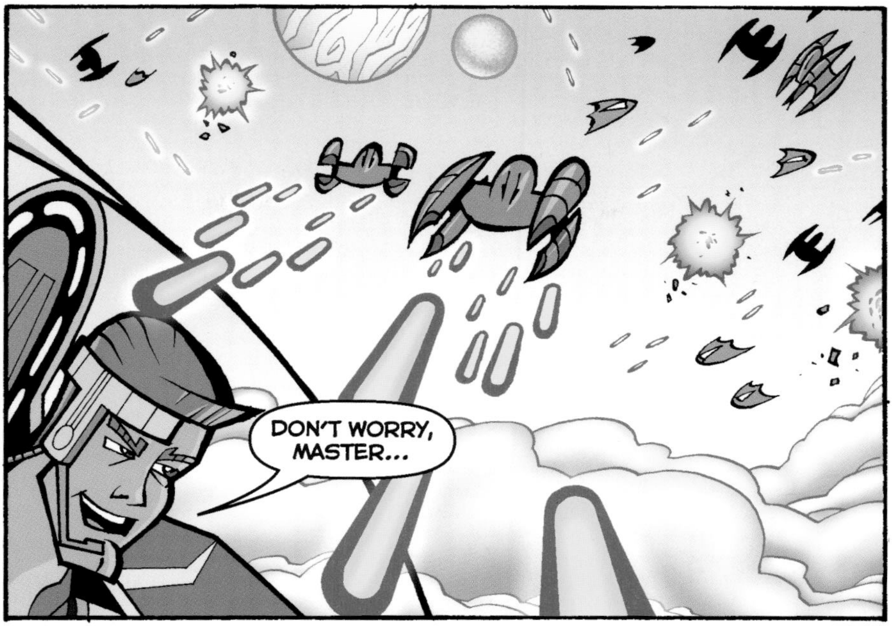
DON'T WORRY, MASTER...

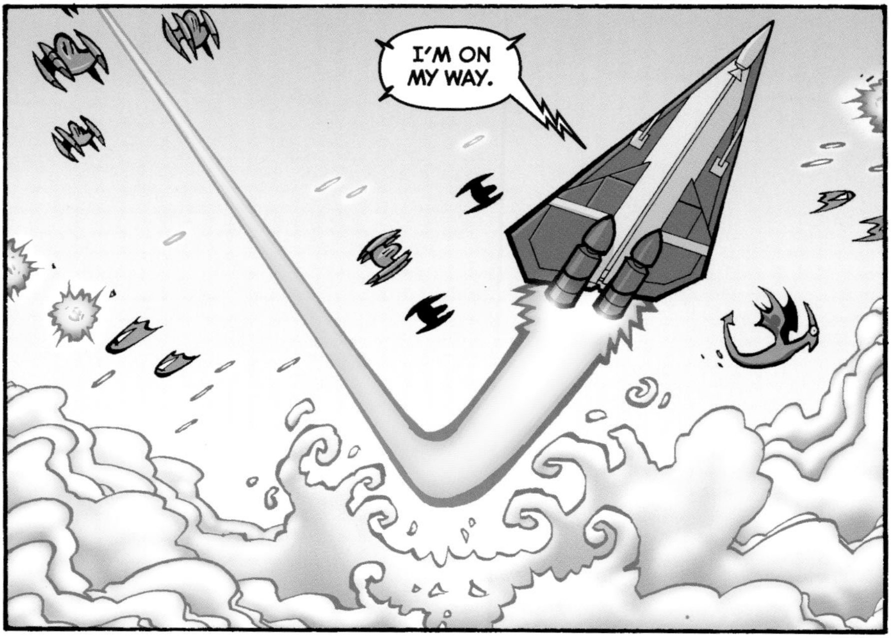
I'M ON MY WAY.

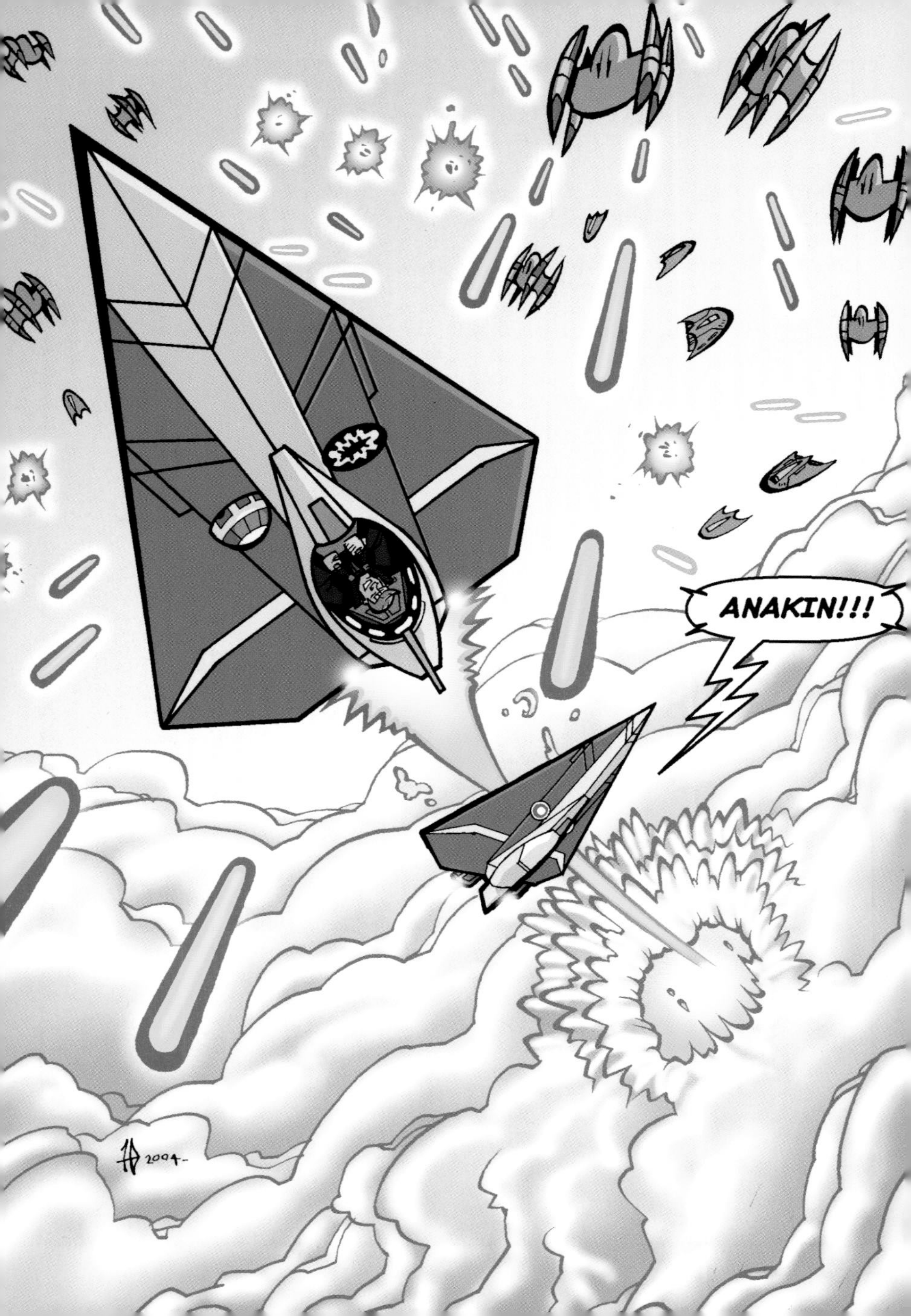
ANAKIN!!!
2004

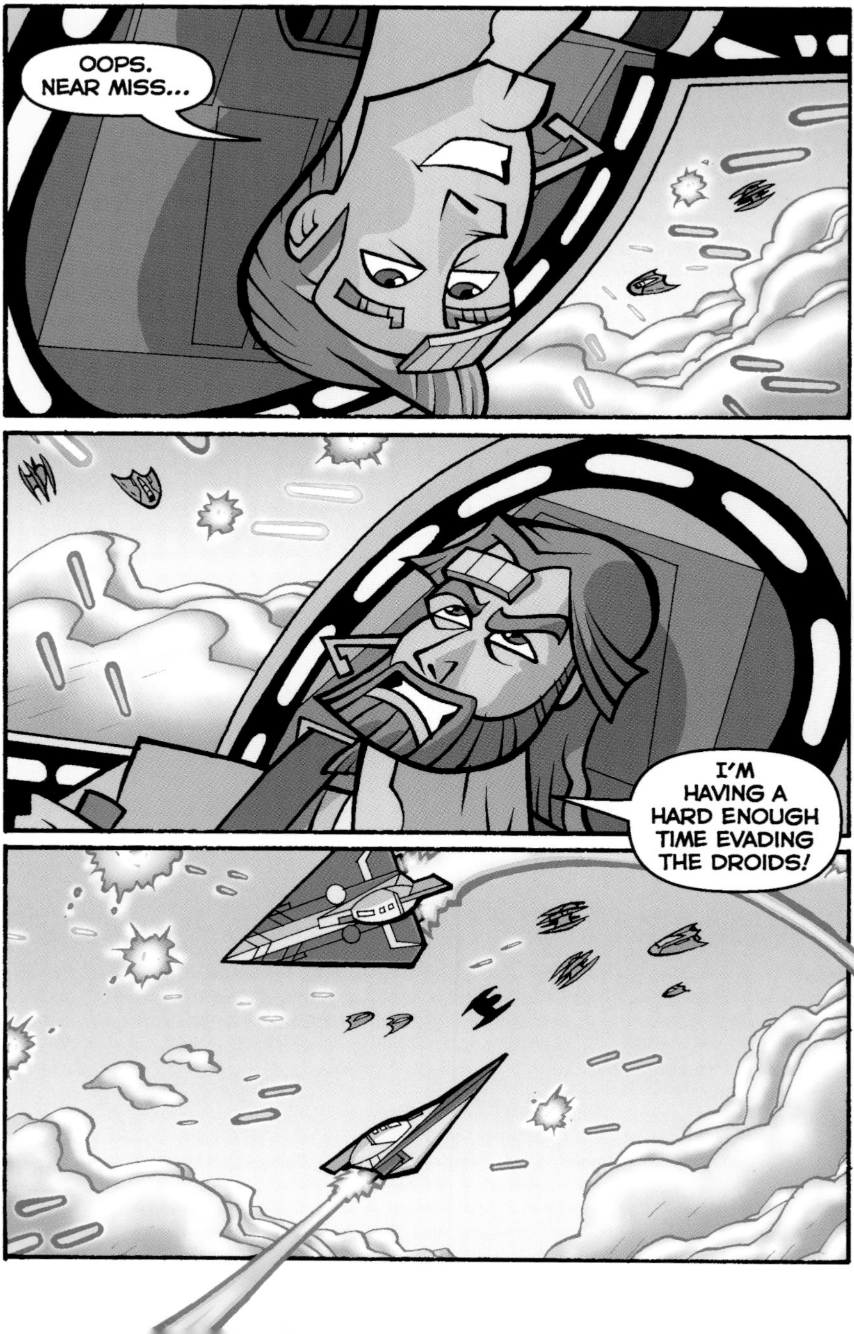
OOPS. NEAR MISS...
I'M HAVING A HARD ENOUGH TIME EVADING THE DROIDS!

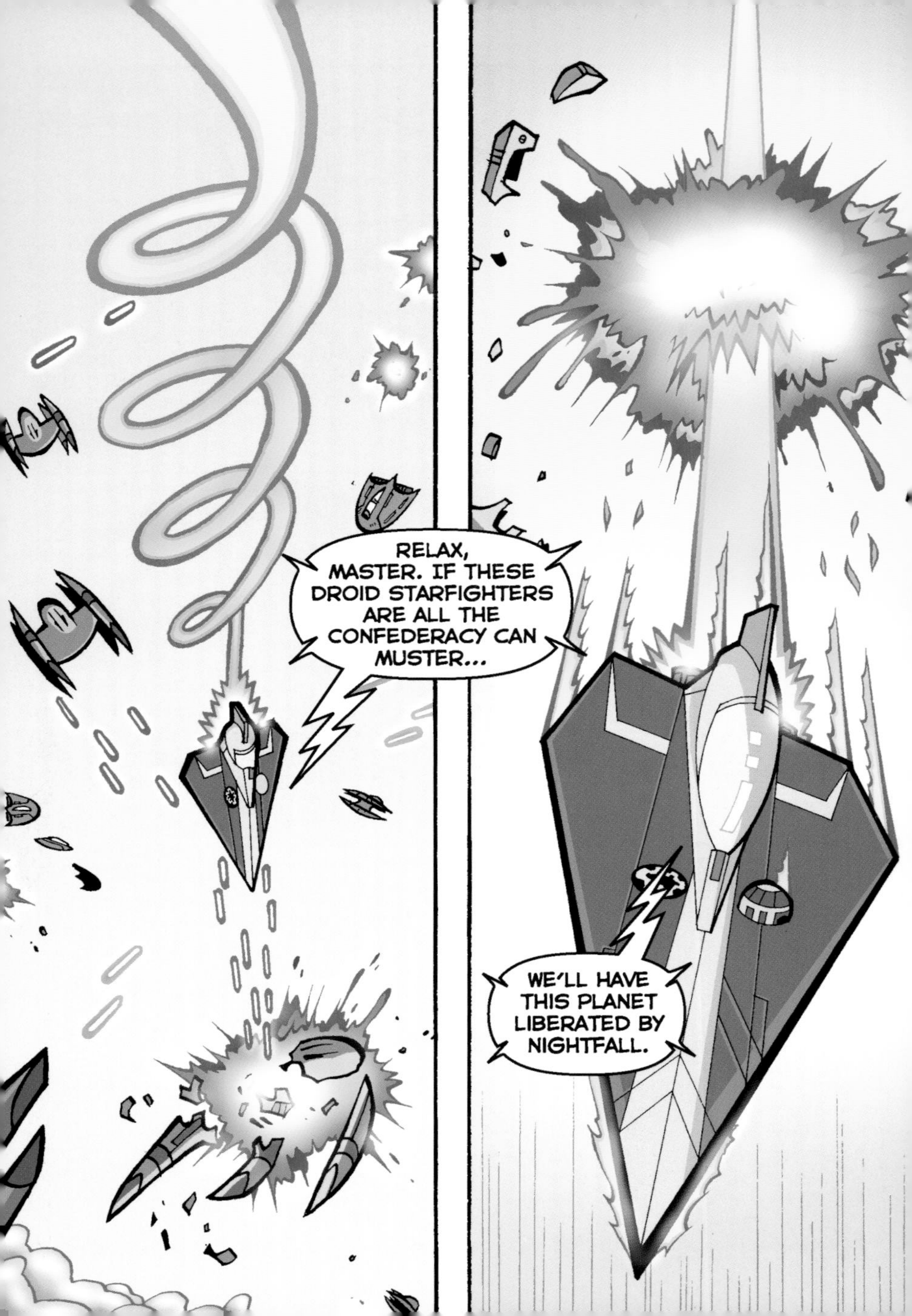
RELAX, MASTER. IF THESE DROID STARFIGHTERS ARE ALL THE CONFEDERACY CAN MUSTER...
WE'LL HAVE THIS PLANET LIBERATED BY NIGHTFALL.

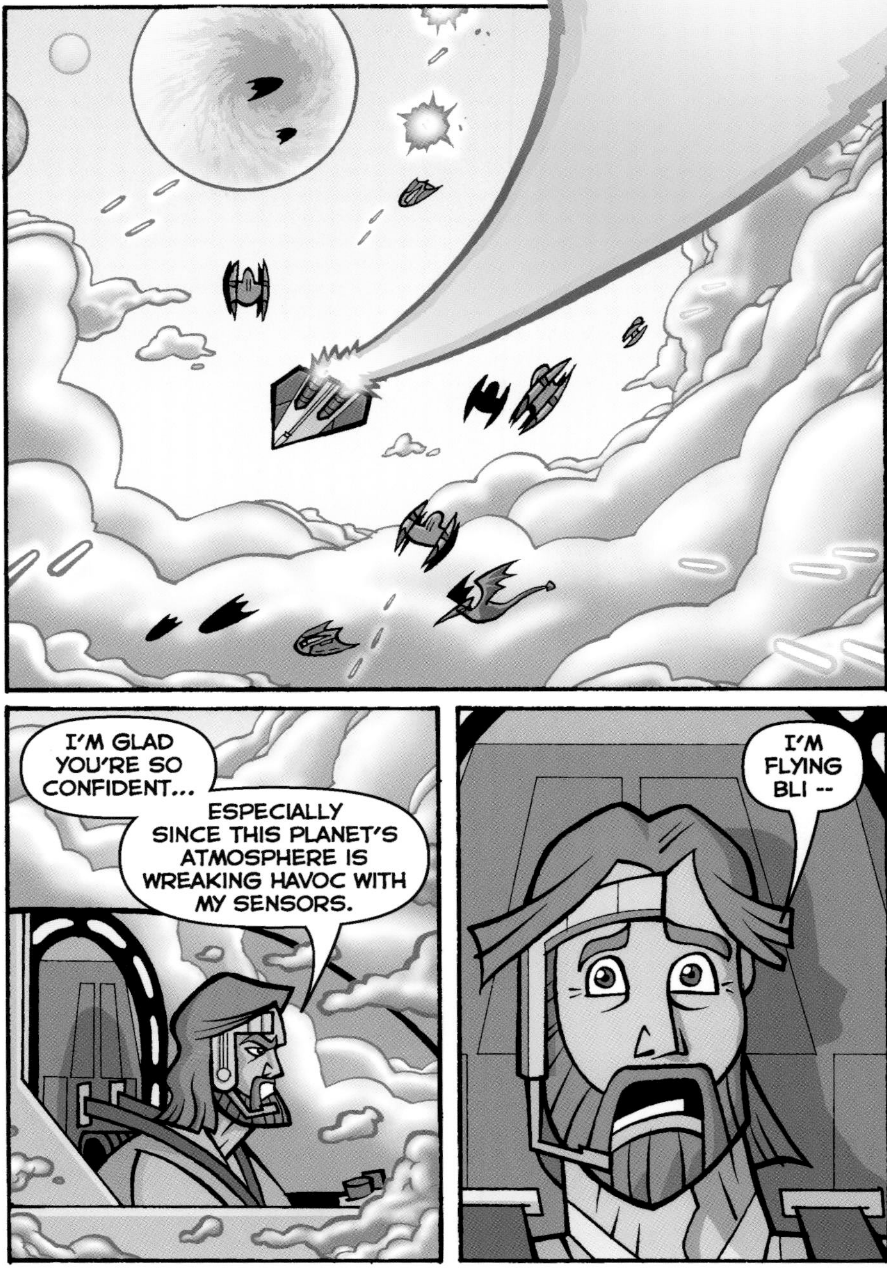
I'M GLAD YOU'RE SO CONFIDENT...
ESPECIALLY SINCE THIS PLANET'S ATMOSPHERE IS WREAKING HAVOC WITH MY SENSORS.
I'M FLYING BLI --

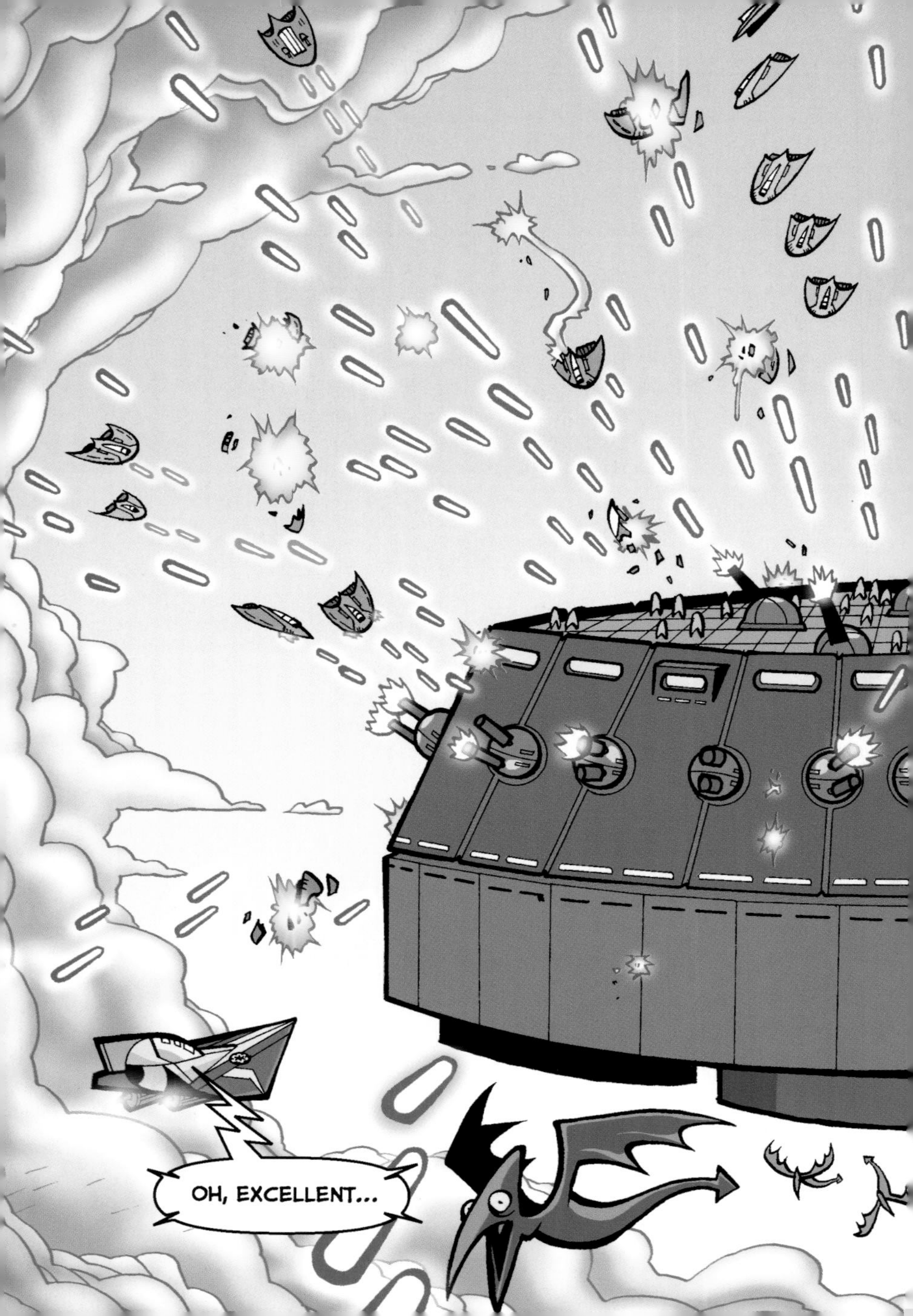
OH, EXCELLENT...

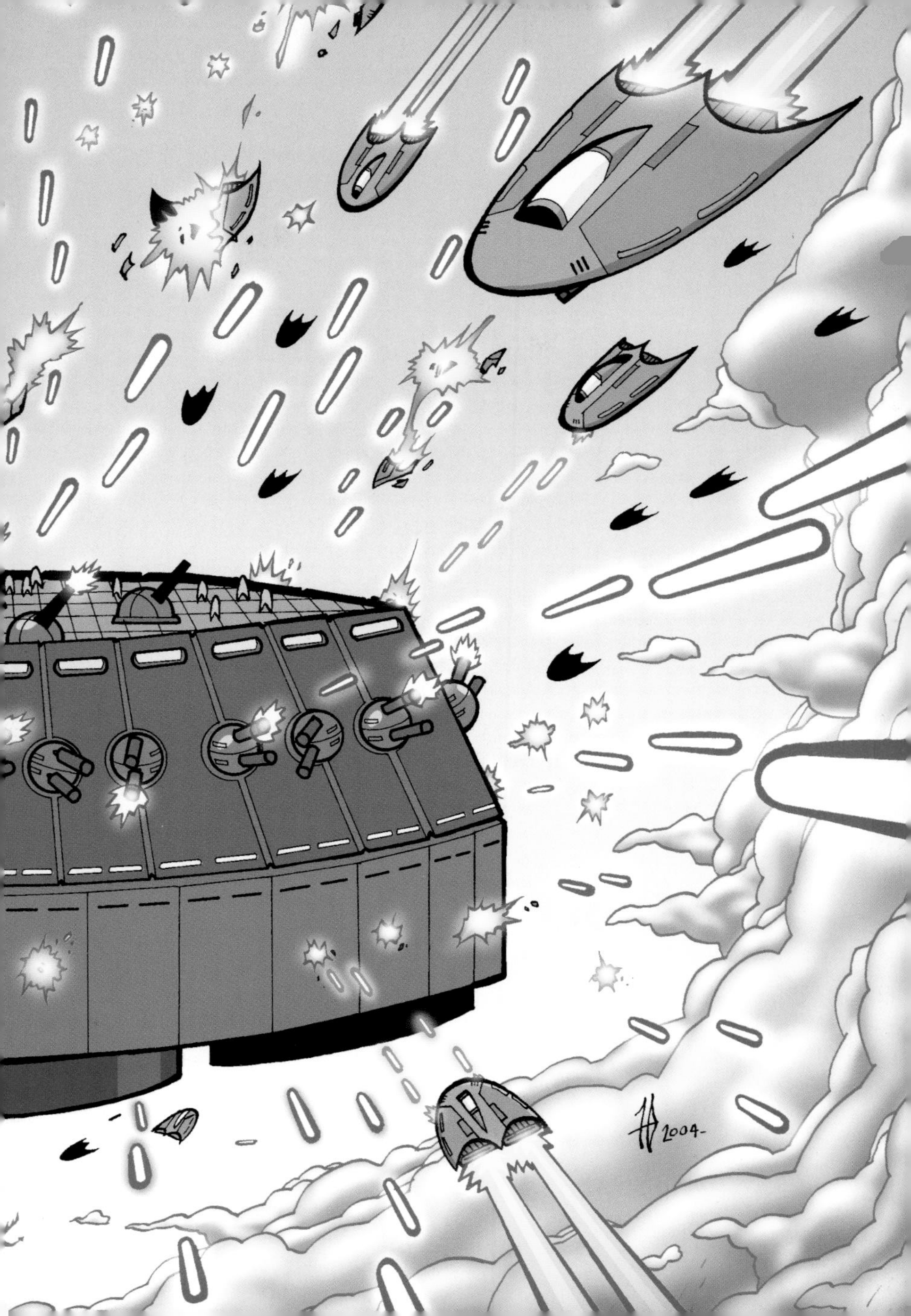
2004-

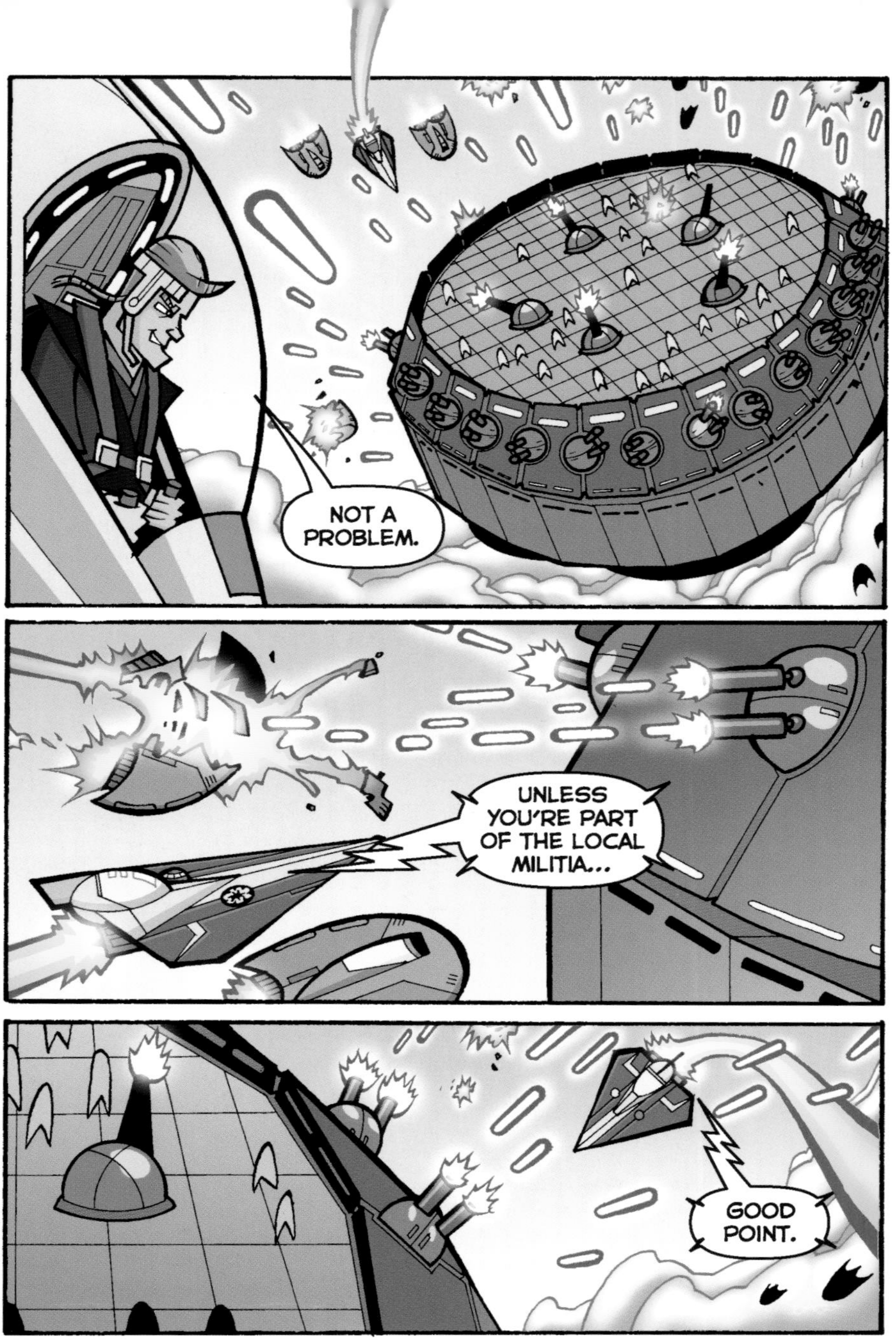
NOT A PROBLEM.
UNLESS YOU'RE PART OF THE LOCAL MILITIA...
GOOD POINT.

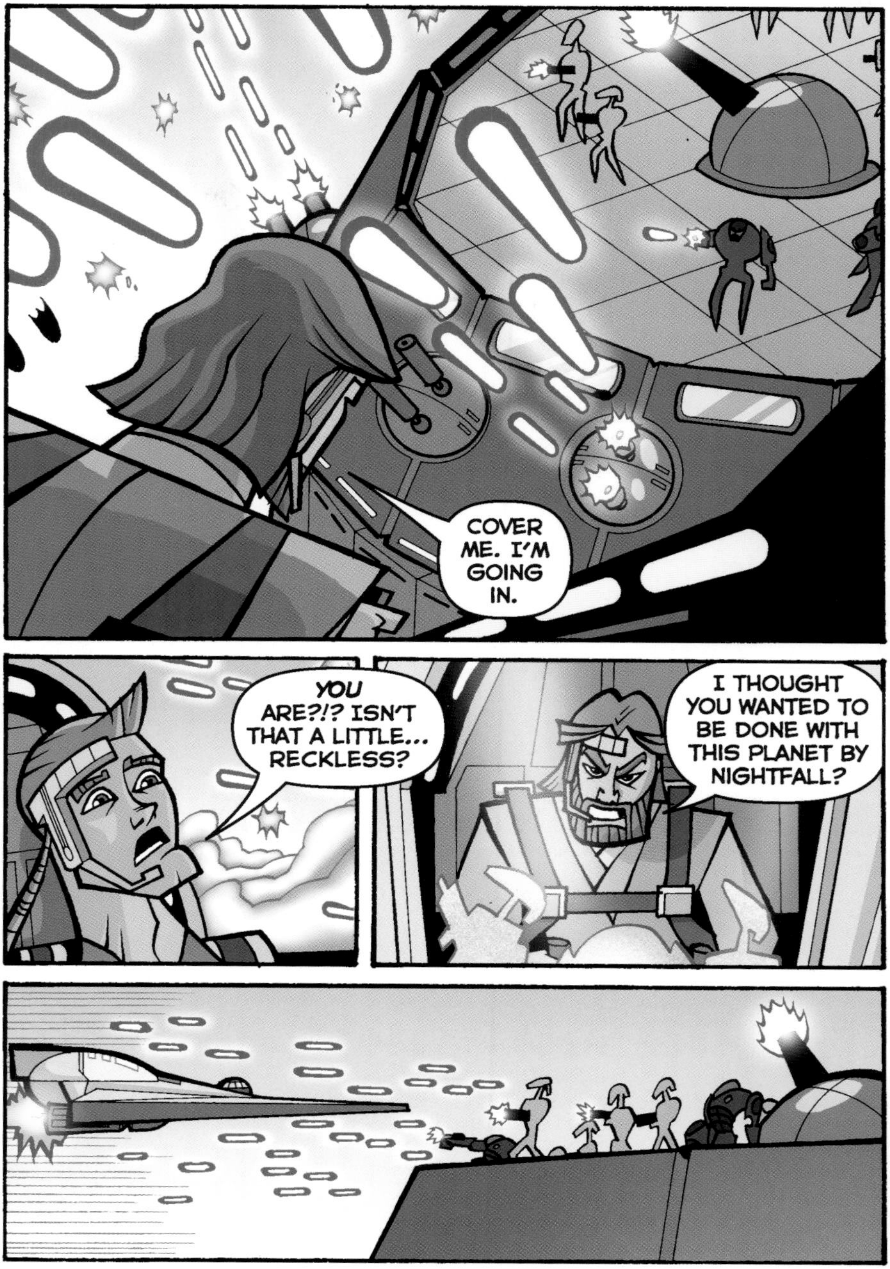
COVER ME. I'M GOING IN.
YOU ARE?!? ISN'T THAT A LITTLE... RECKLESS?
I THOUGHT YOU WANTED TO BE DONE WITH THIS PLANET BY NIGHTFALL?

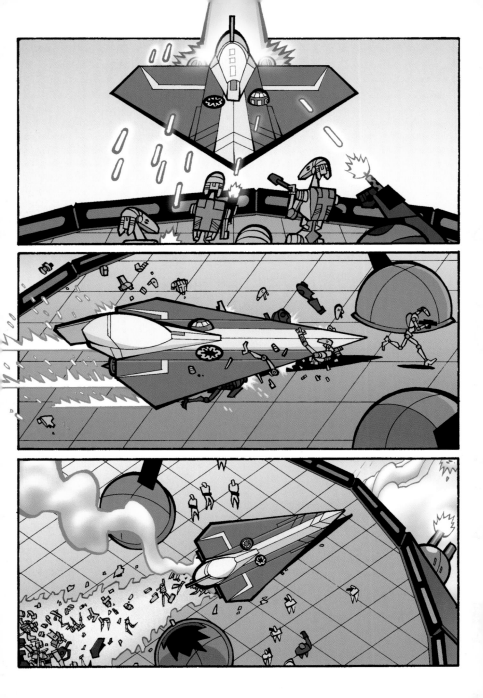

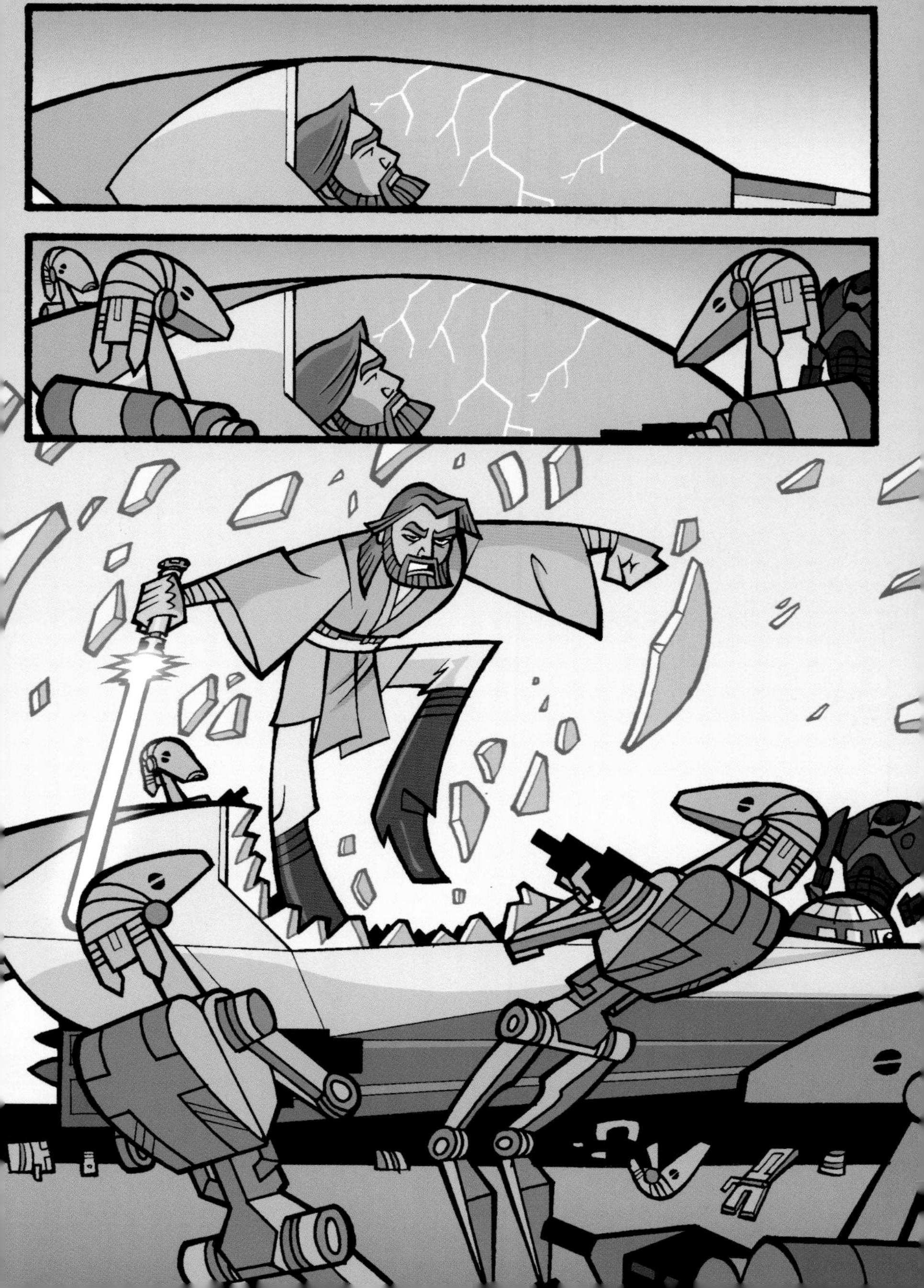

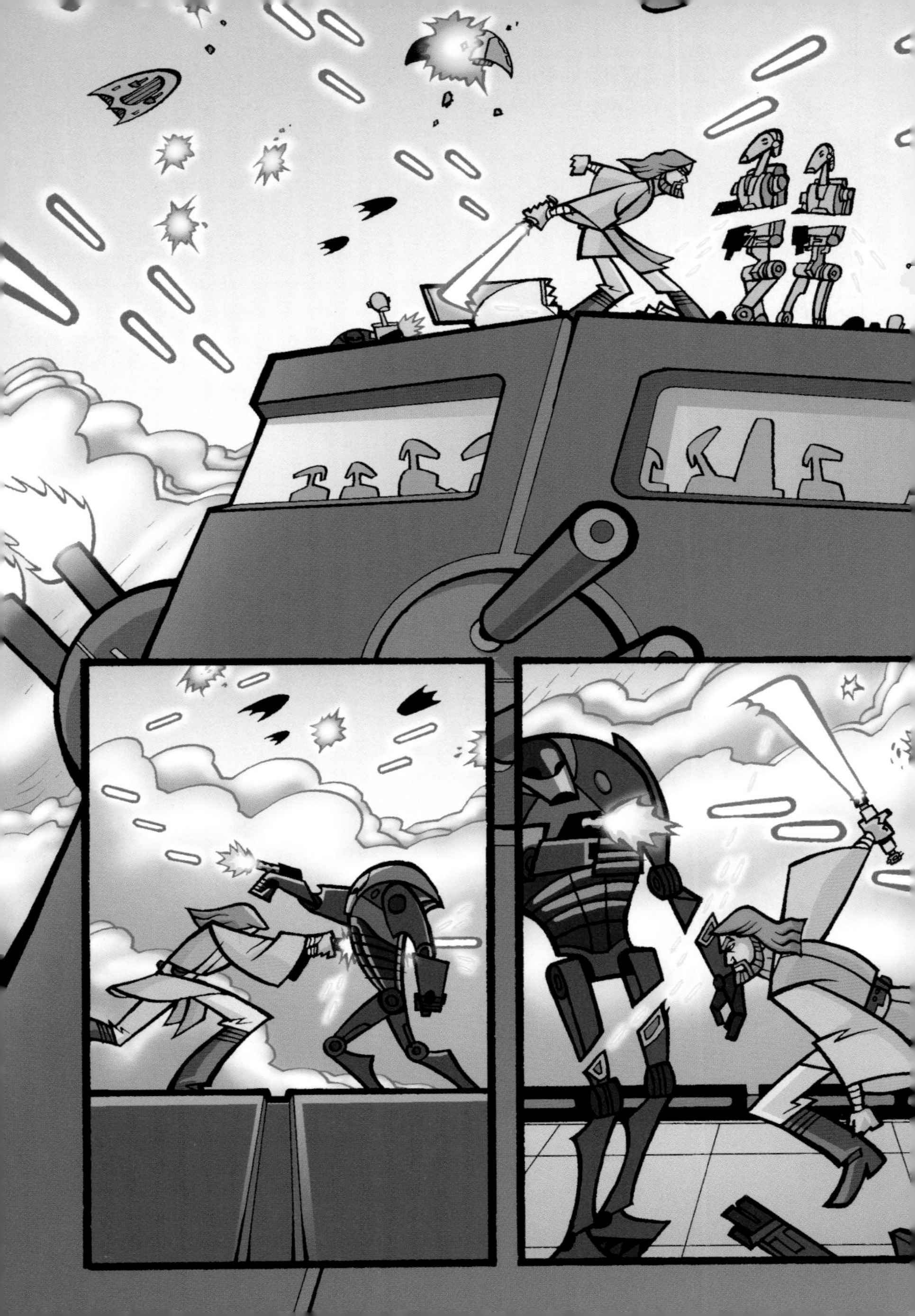

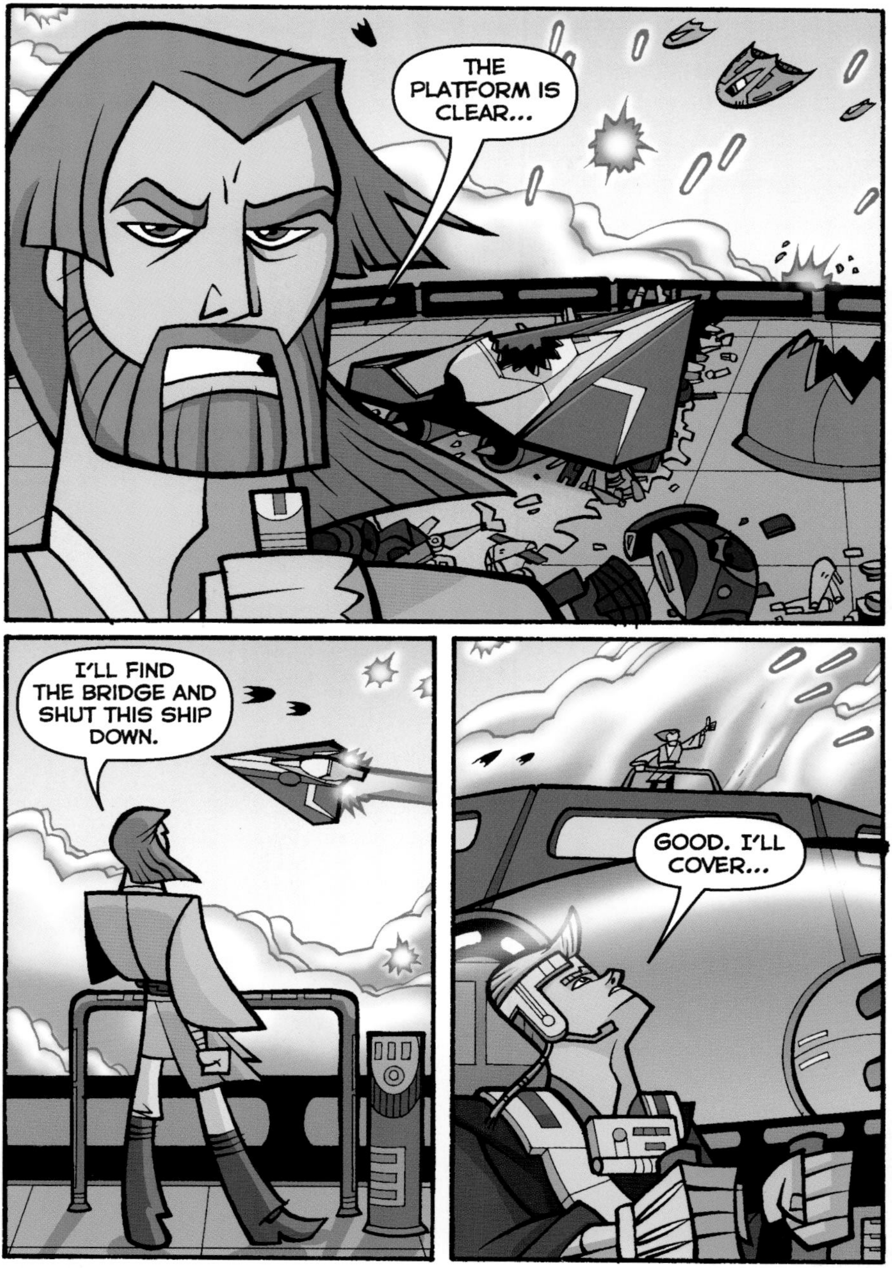
THE PLATFORM IS CLEAR...
I'LL FIND THE BRIDGE AND SHUT THIS SHIP DOWN.
GOOD. I'LL COVER...

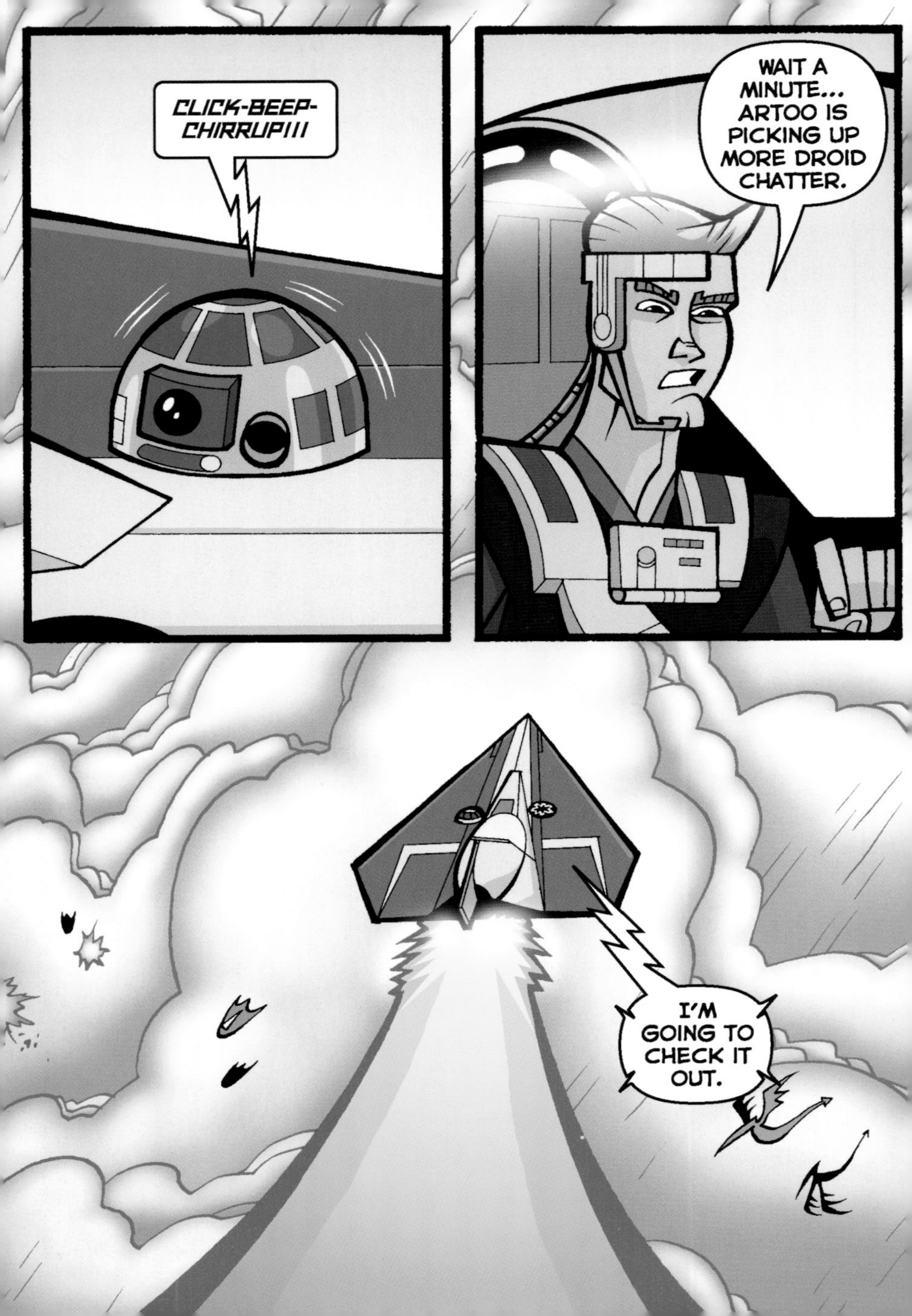
CLICK-BEEP-CHIRRUP!!!
WAIT A MINUTE... ARTOO IS PICKING UP MORE DROID CHATTER.
I'M GOING TO CHECK IT OUT.

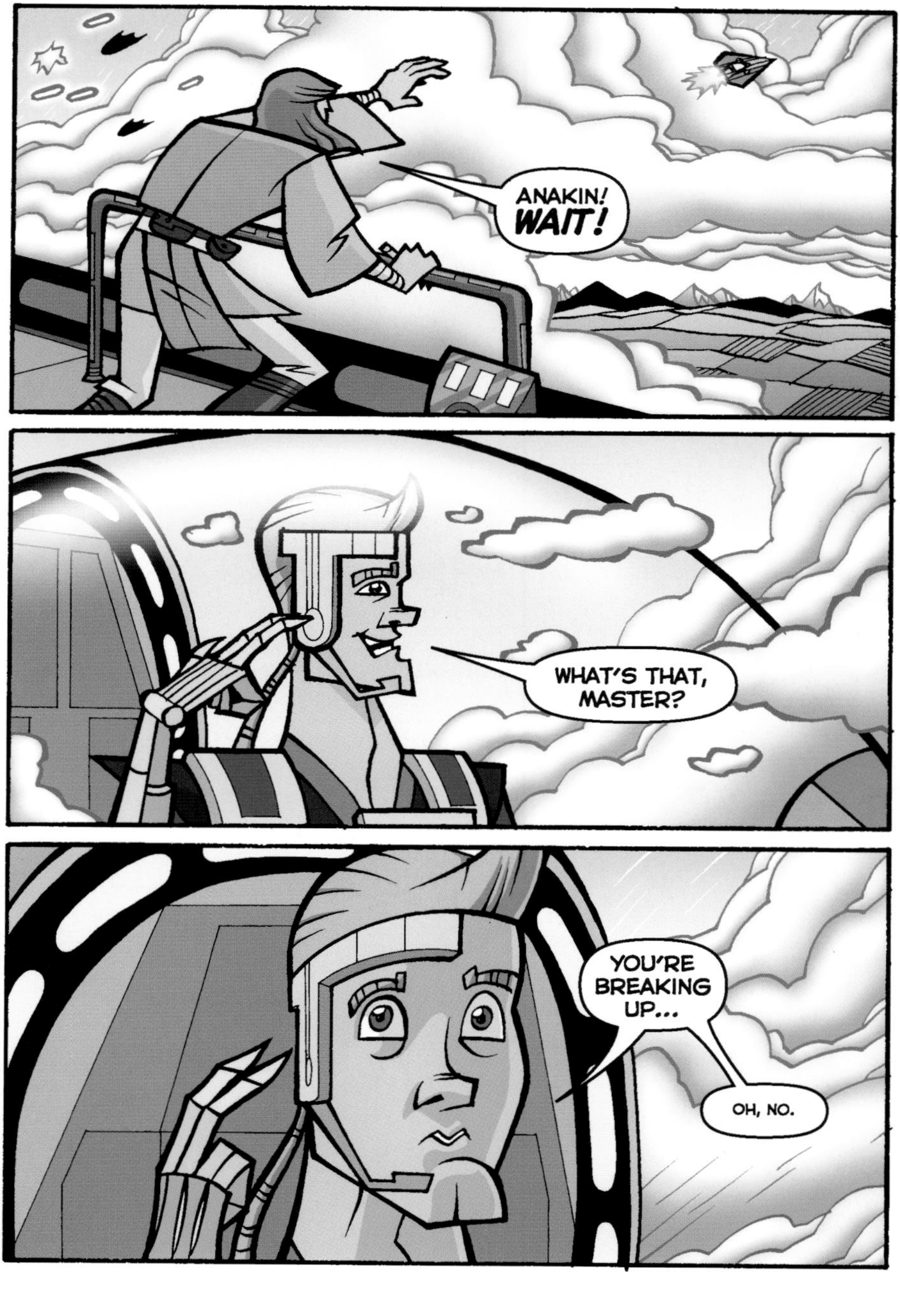
ANAKIN! WAIT!
WHAT'S THAT, MASTER?
YOU'RE BREAKING UP...
OH, NO.

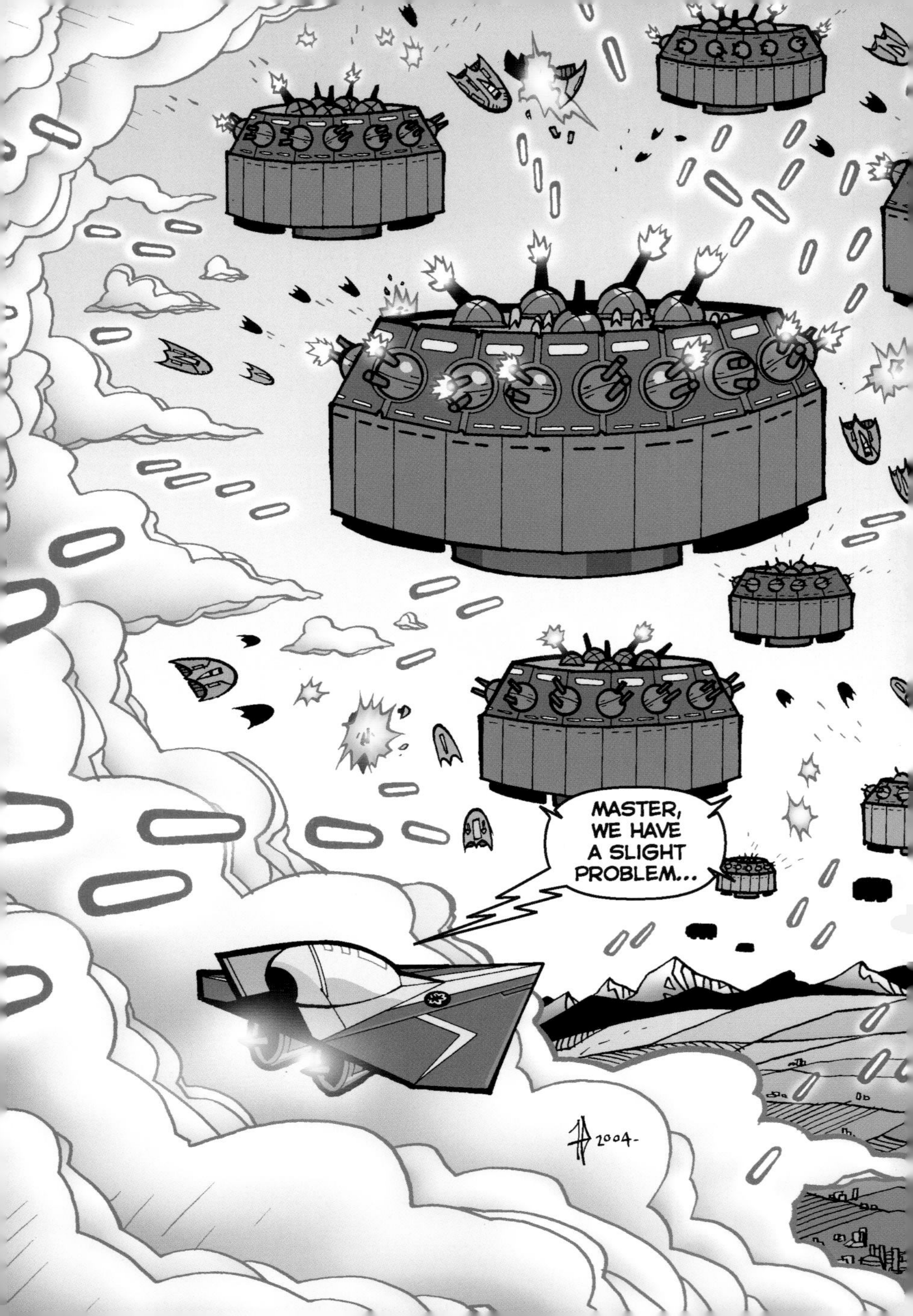
MASTER, WE HAVE A SLIGHT PROBLEM...
2004-

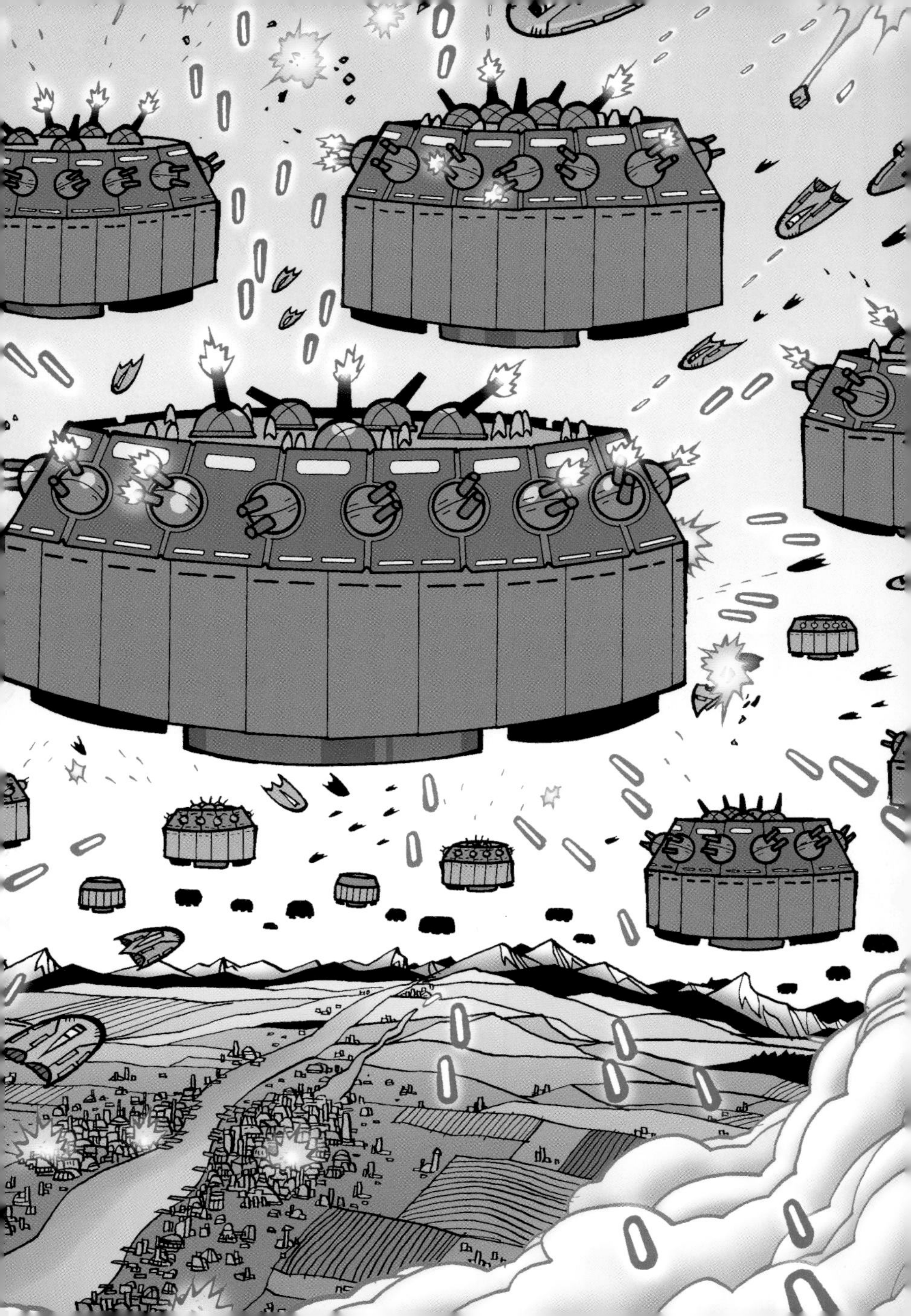

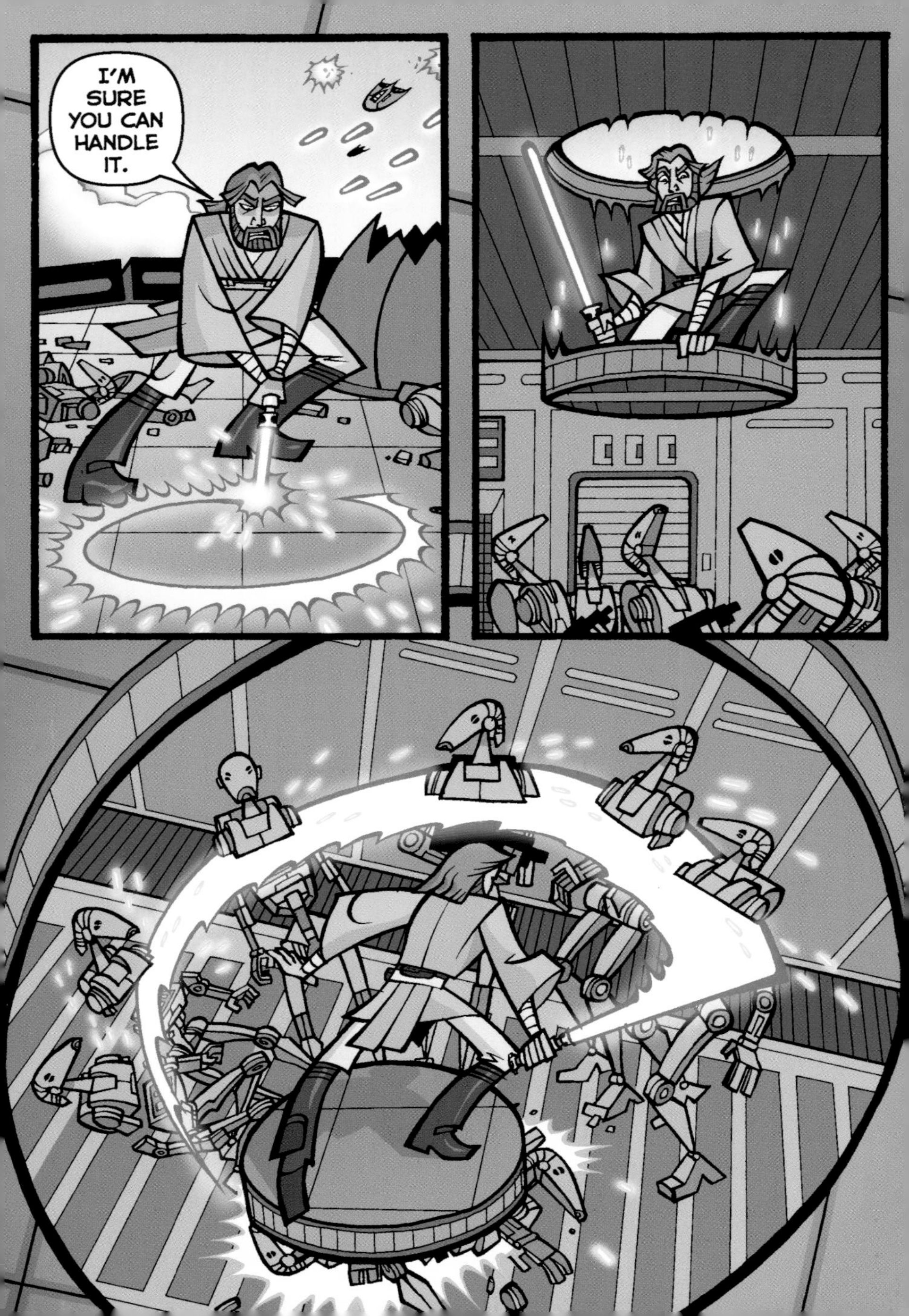
I'M SURE YOU CAN HANDLE IT.

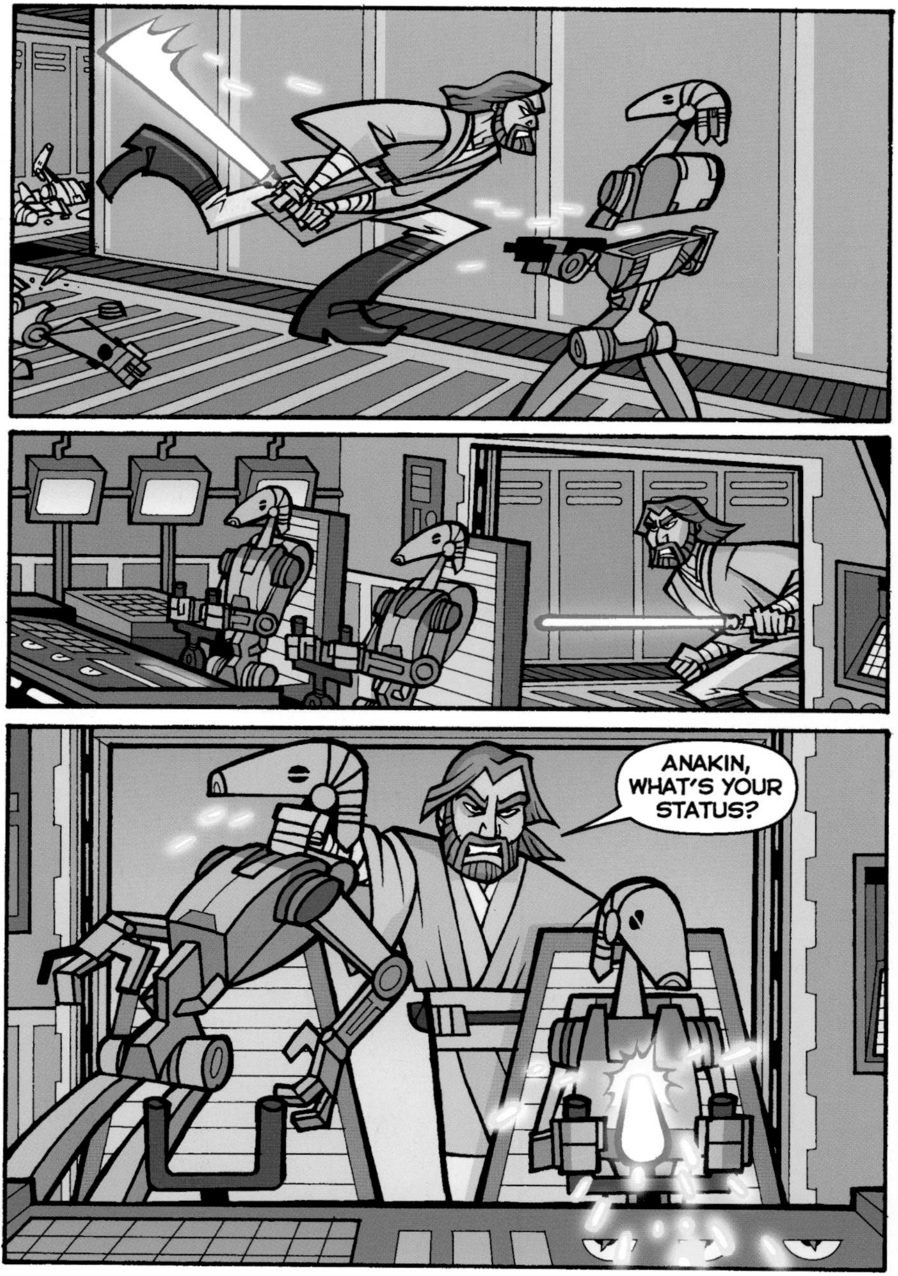
ANAKIN, WHAT'S YOUR STATUS?

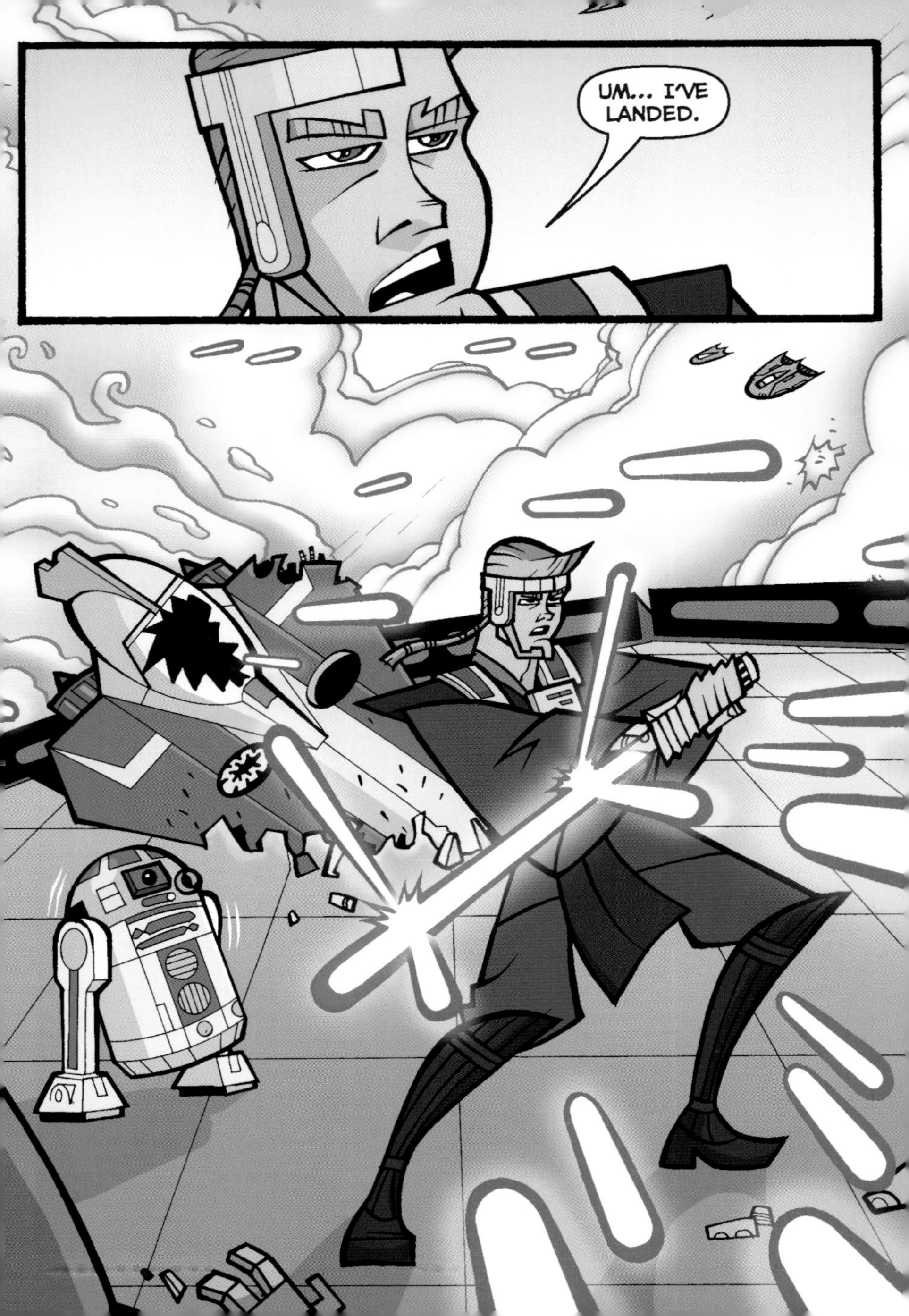
UM... I'VE LANDED.

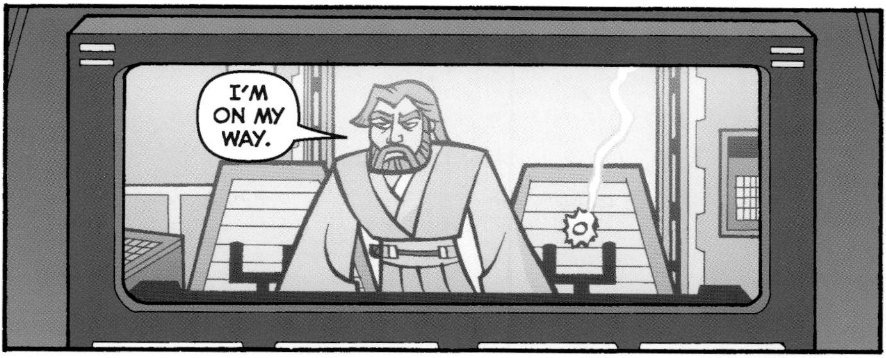
I'M ON MY WAY.

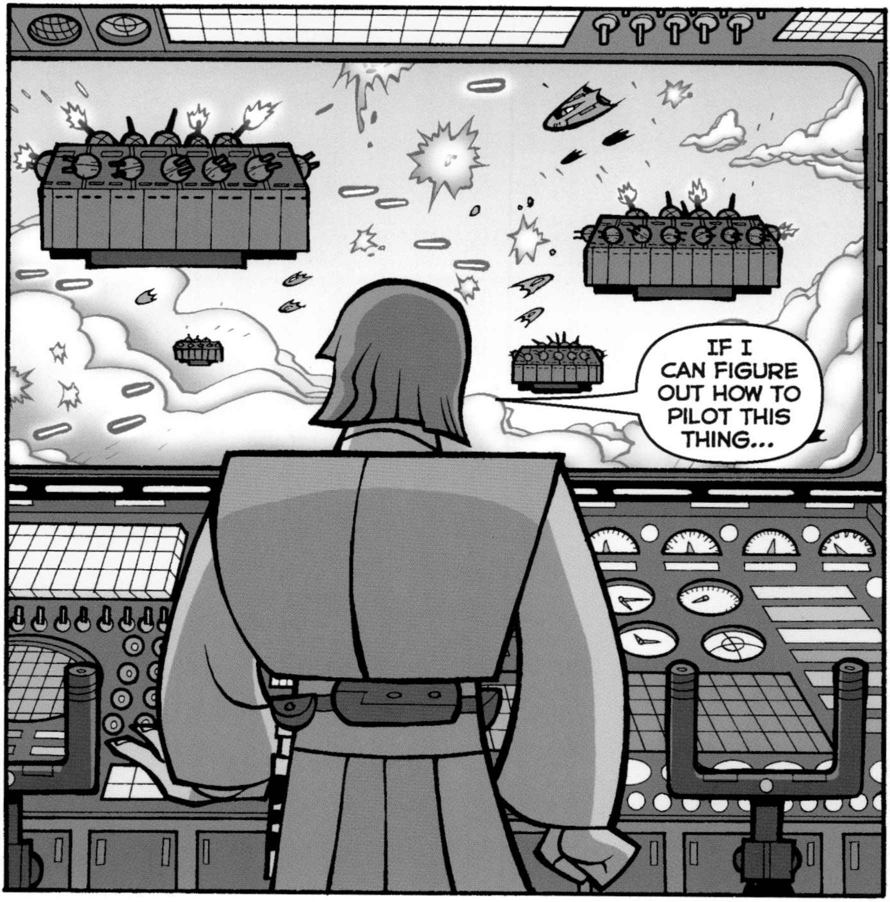
IF I CAN FIGURE OUT HOW TO PILOT THIS THING...

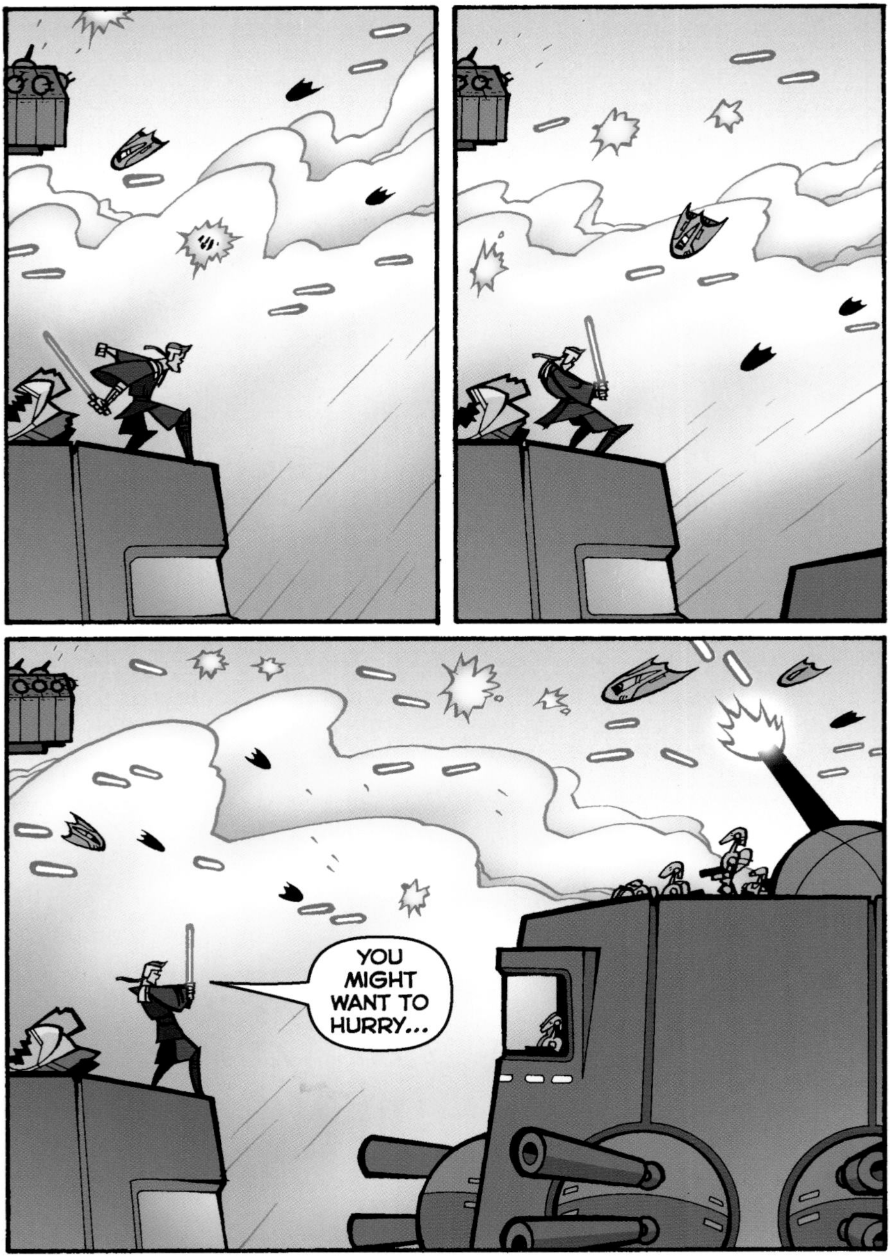
YOU MIGHT WANT TO HURRY...

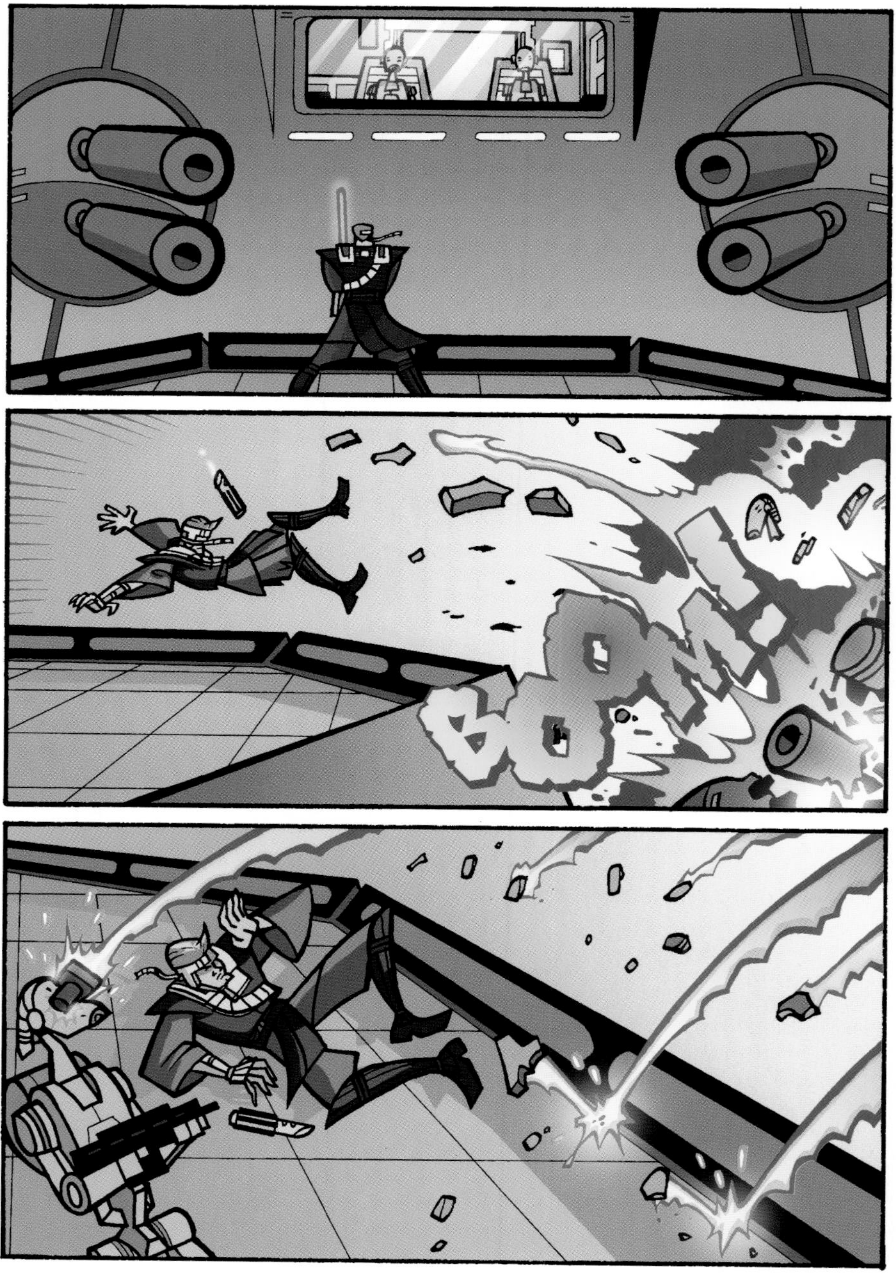
BOOM

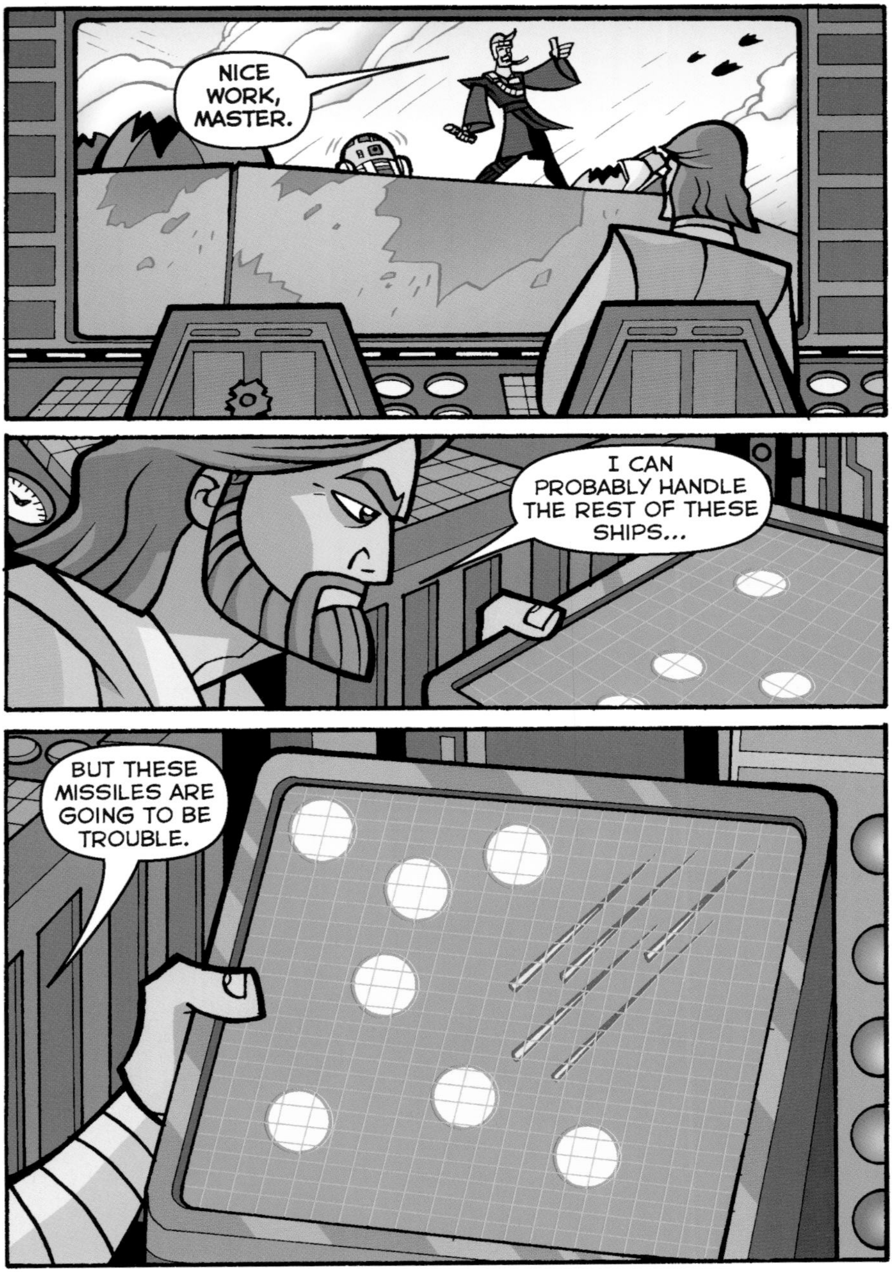
NICE WORK, MASTER.
I CAN PROBABLY HANDLE THE REST OF THESE SHIPS...
BUT THESE MISSILES ARE GOING TO BE TROUBLE.

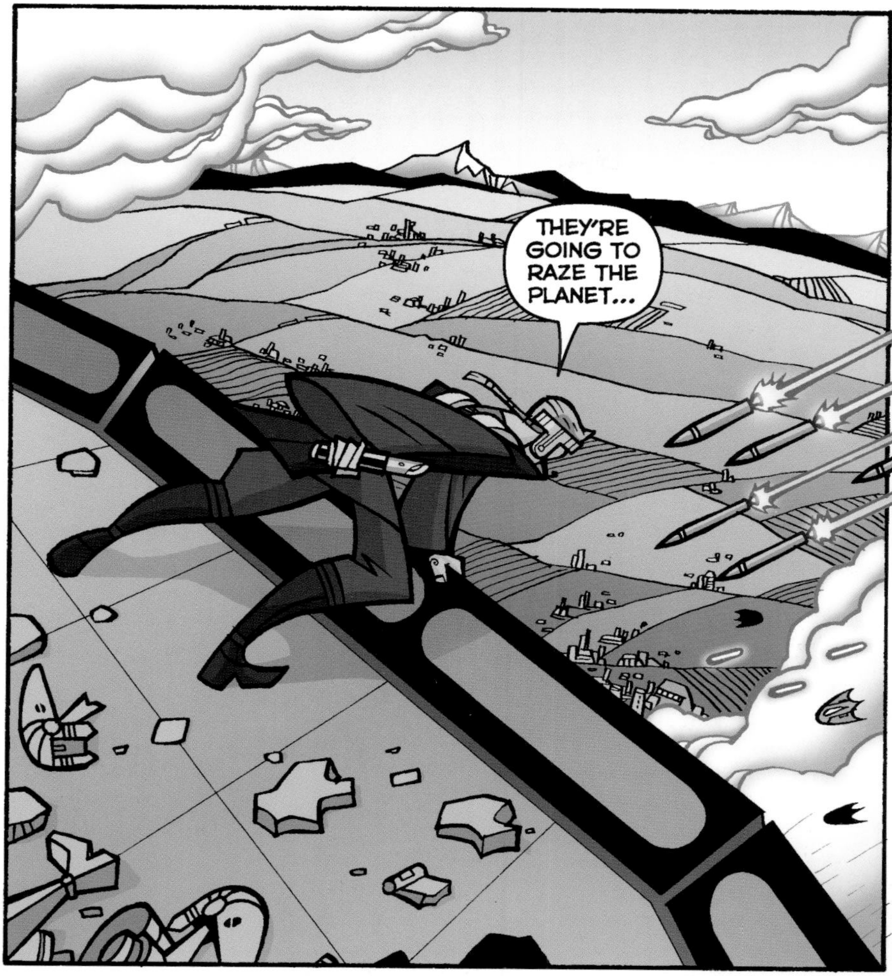
THEY'RE GOING TO RAZE THE PLANET...

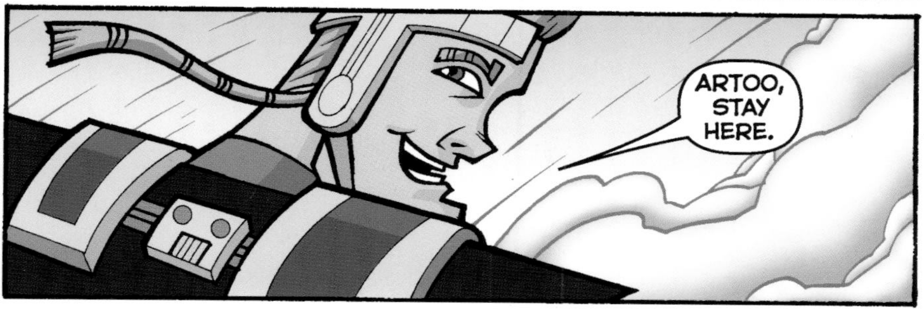
ARTOO, STAY HERE.

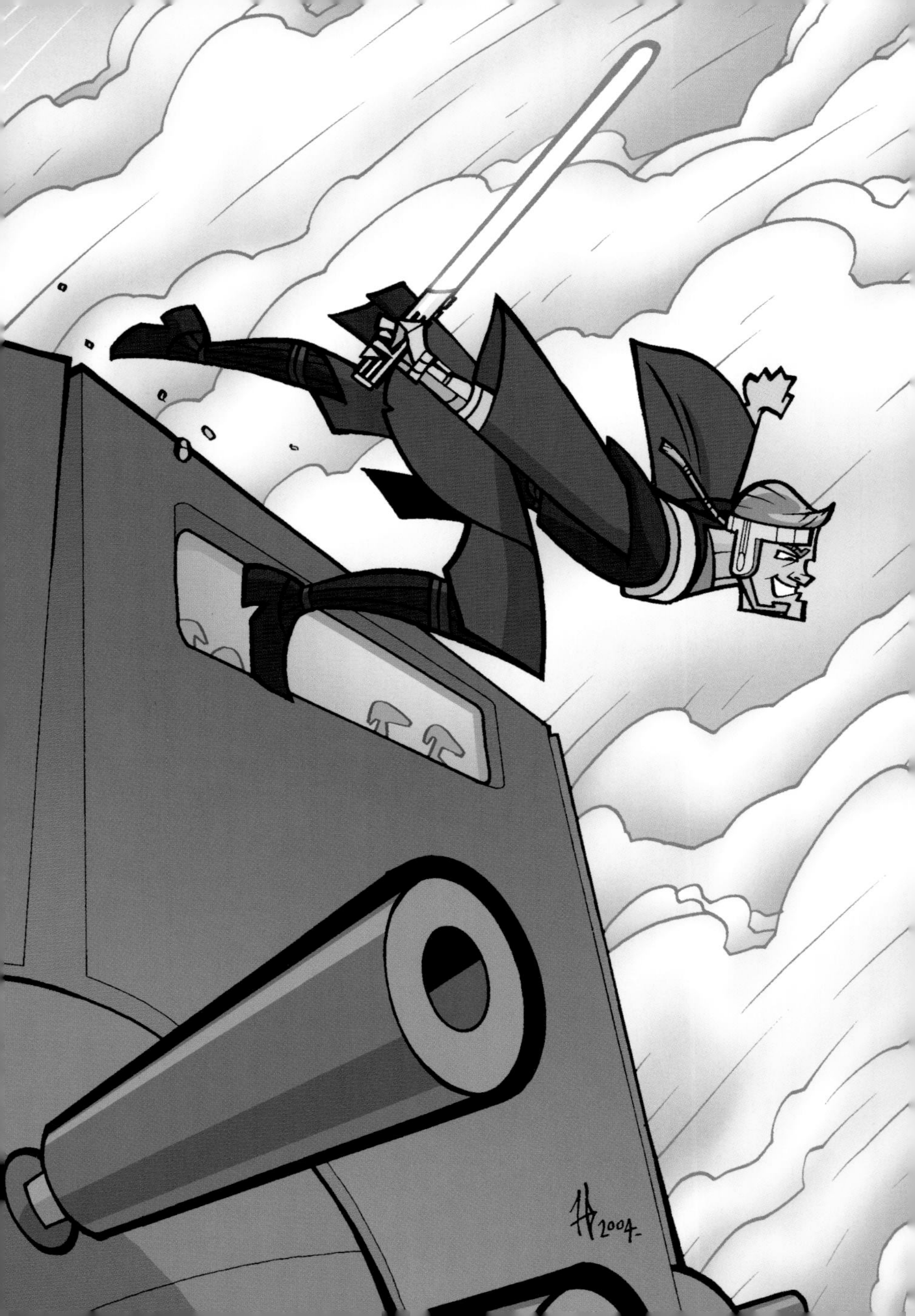

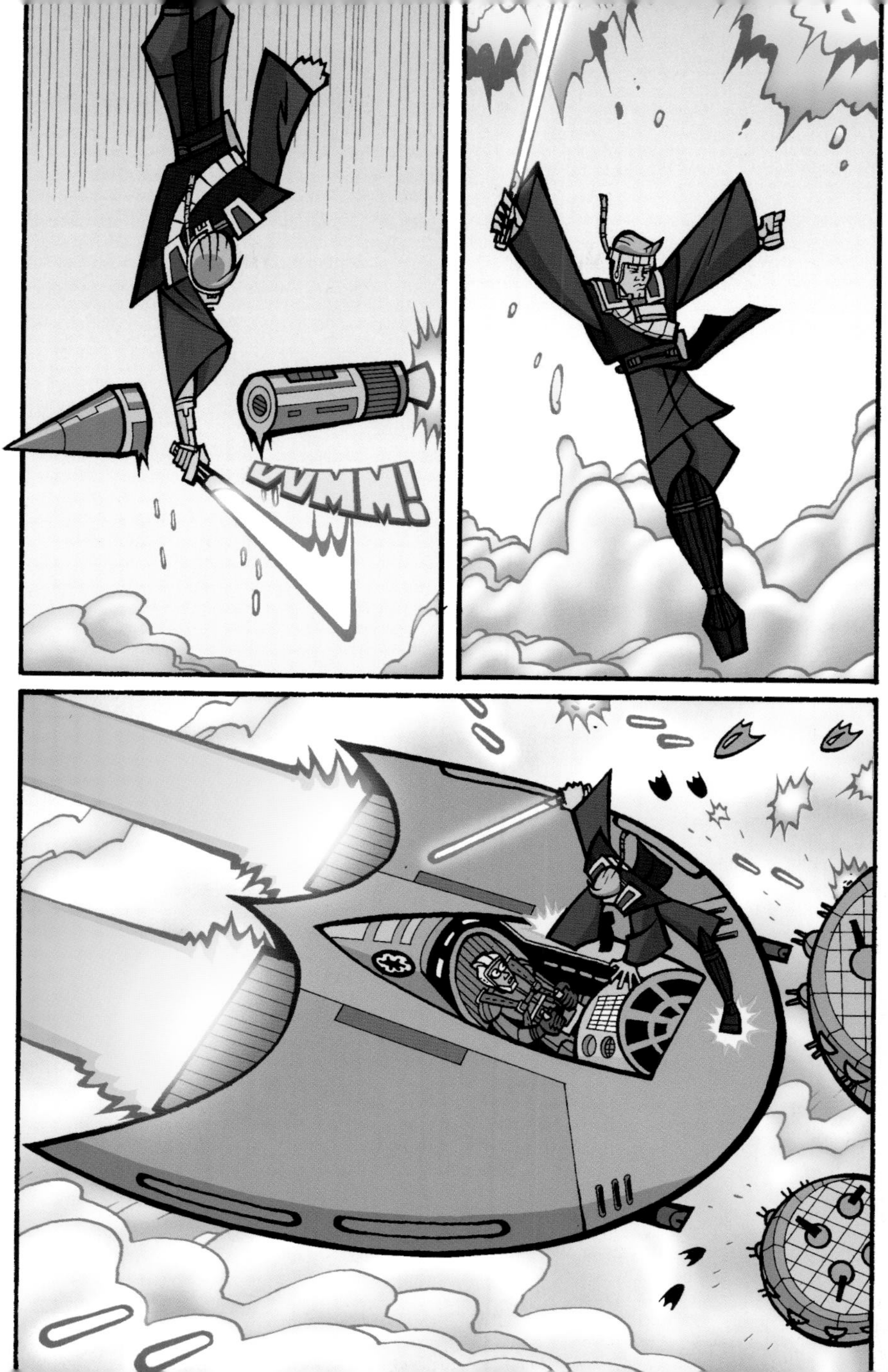
VVMM!

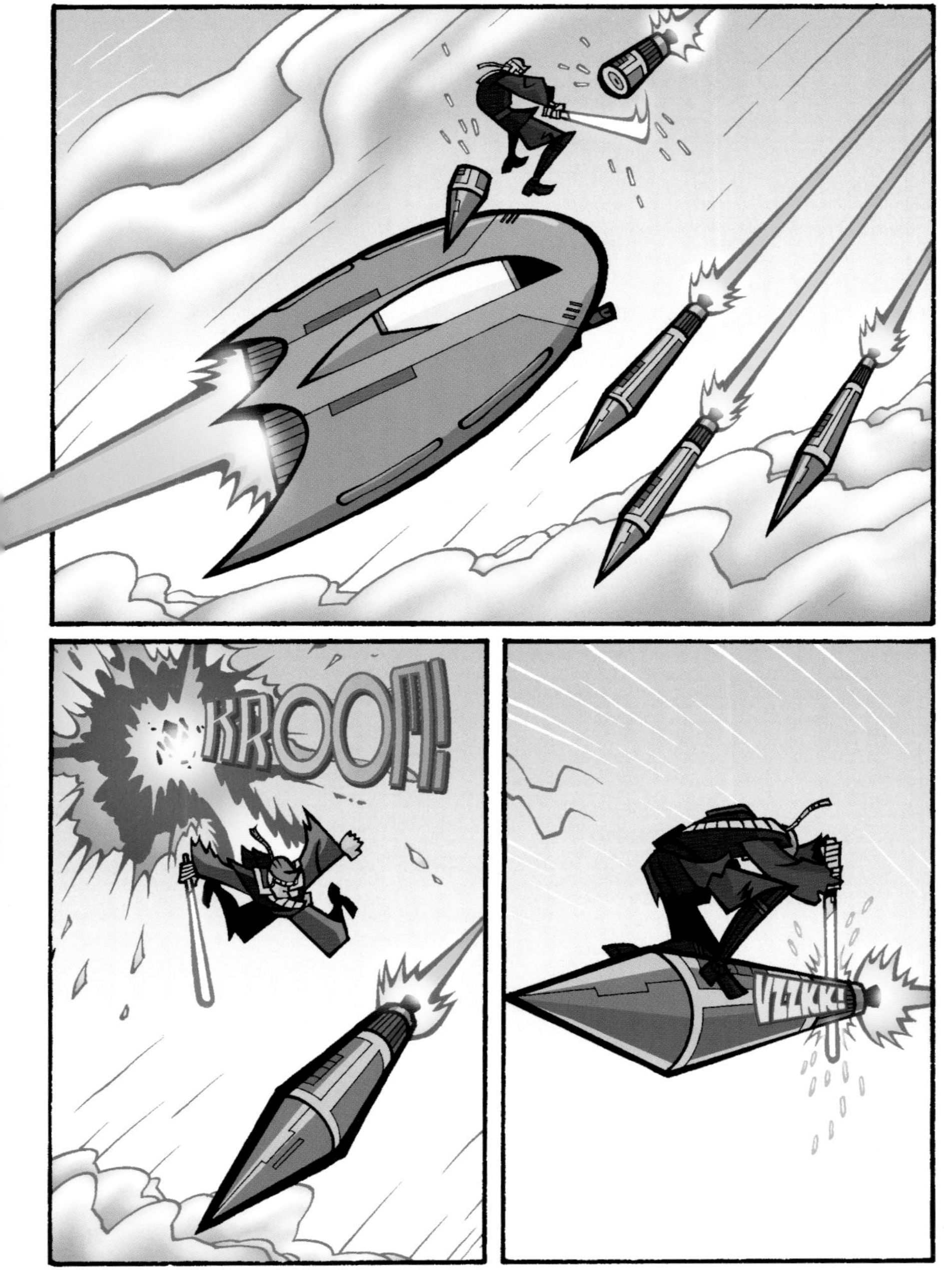
KROOM!
VZZKK!

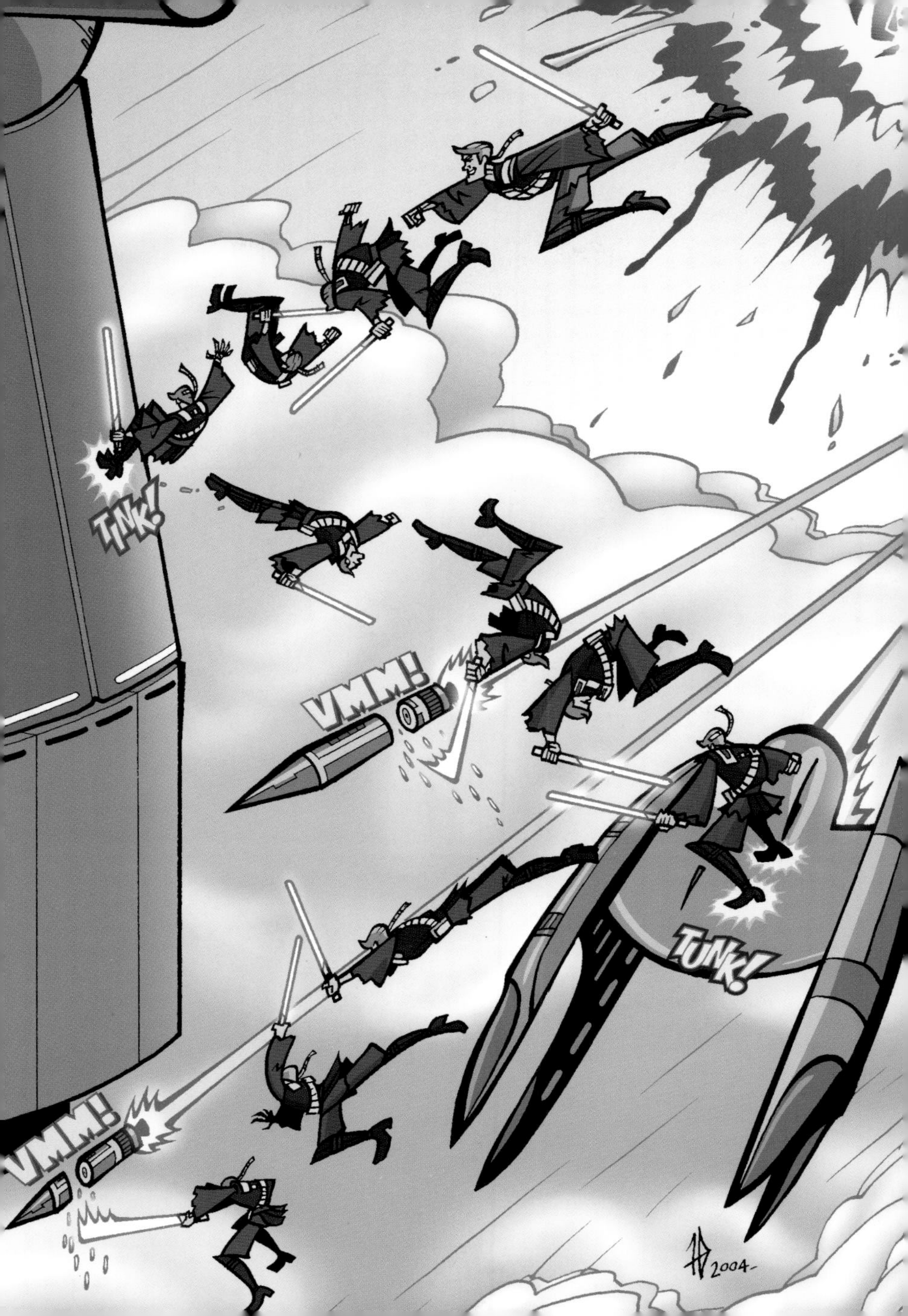
TINK!
VMM!
TUNK!
VMM!
2004

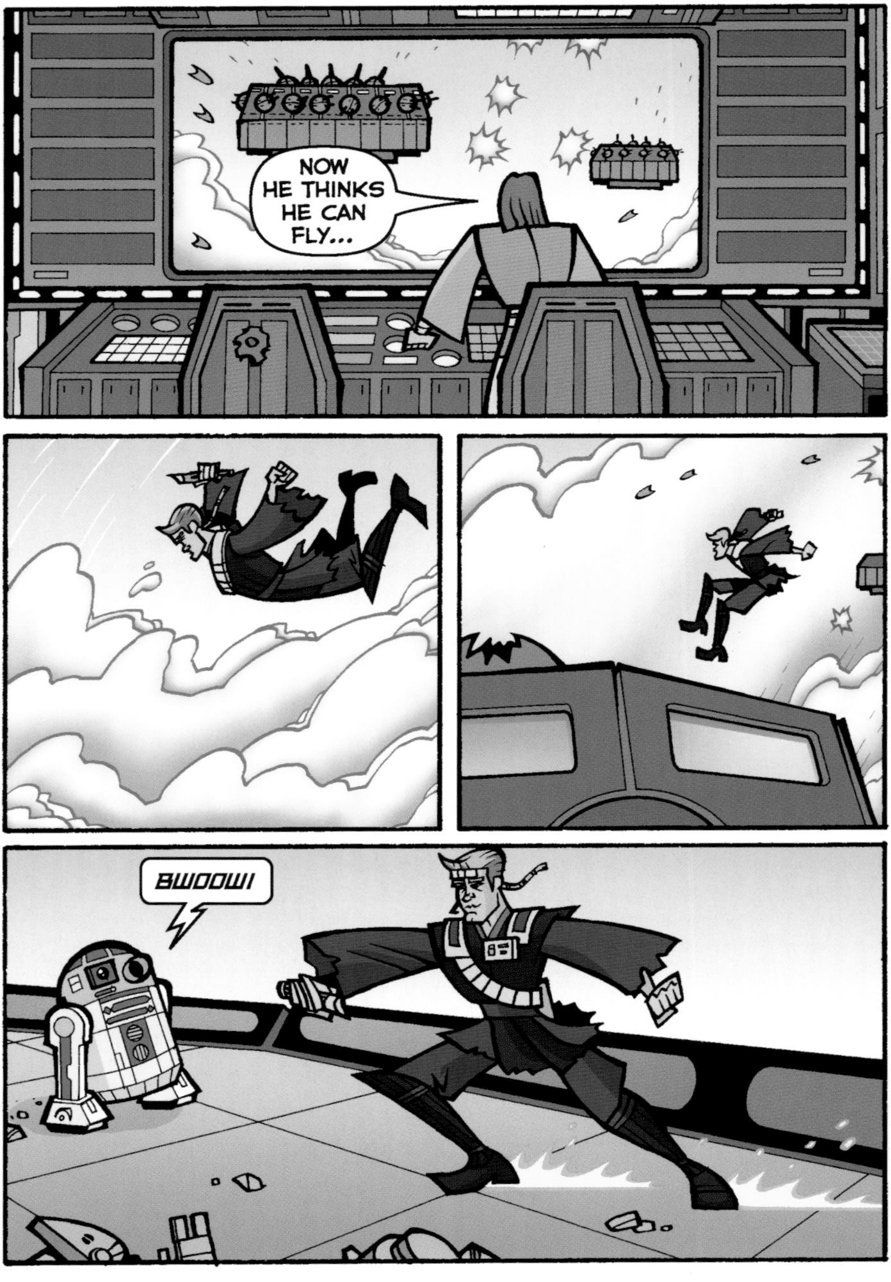
NOW HE THINKS HE CAN FLY...
BWOOWI

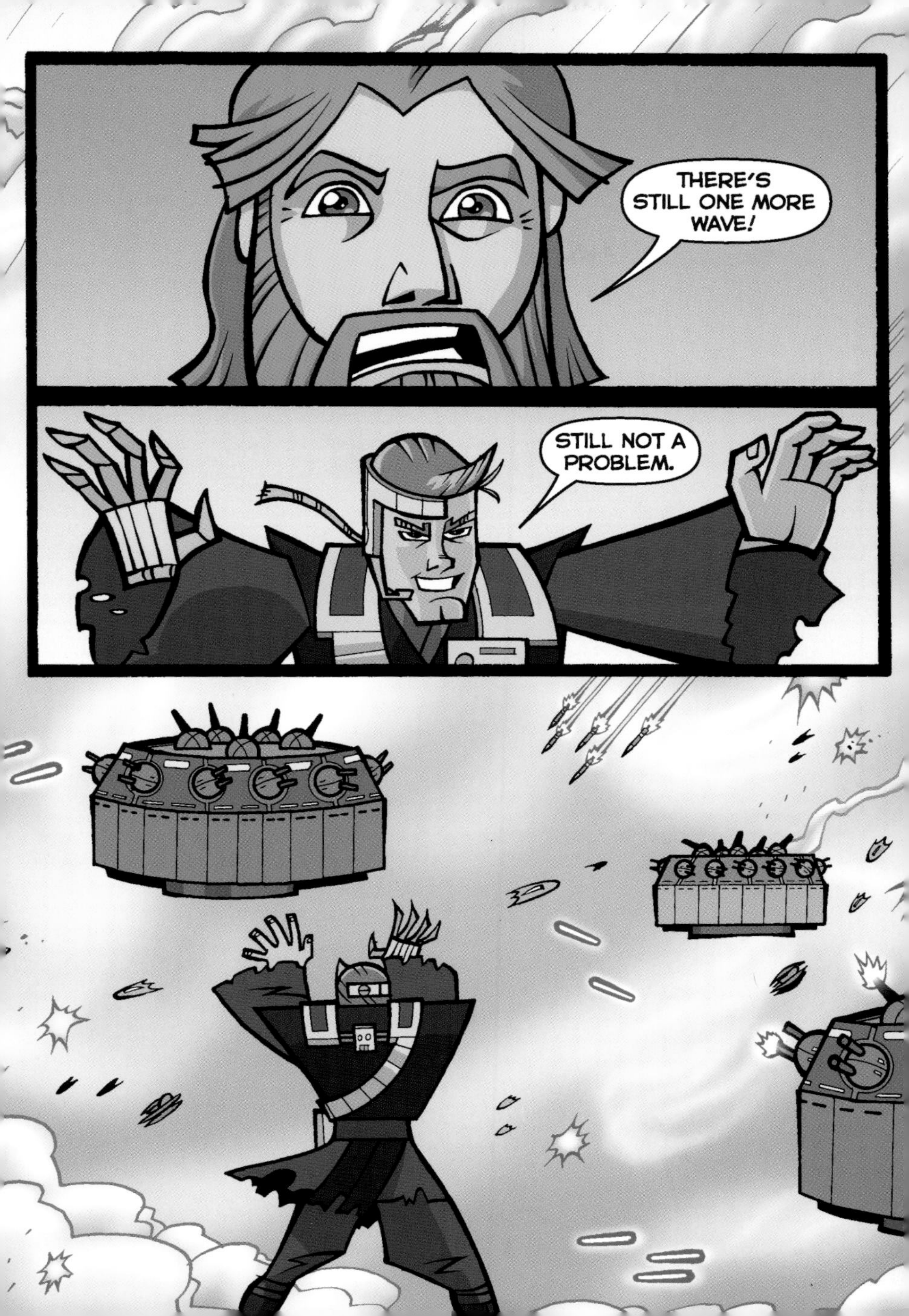
THERE'S STILL ONE MORE WAVE!
STILL NOT A PROBLEM.

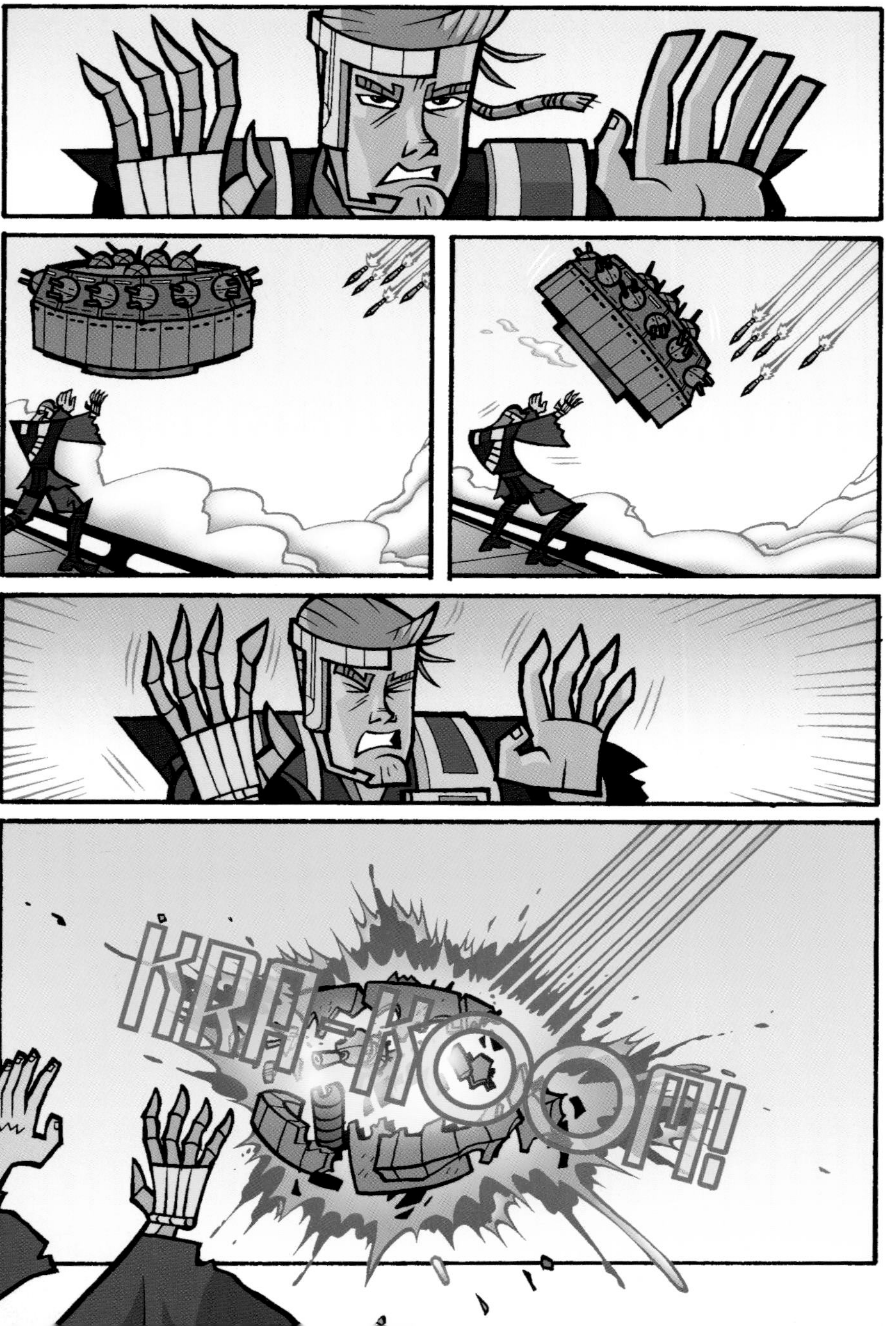

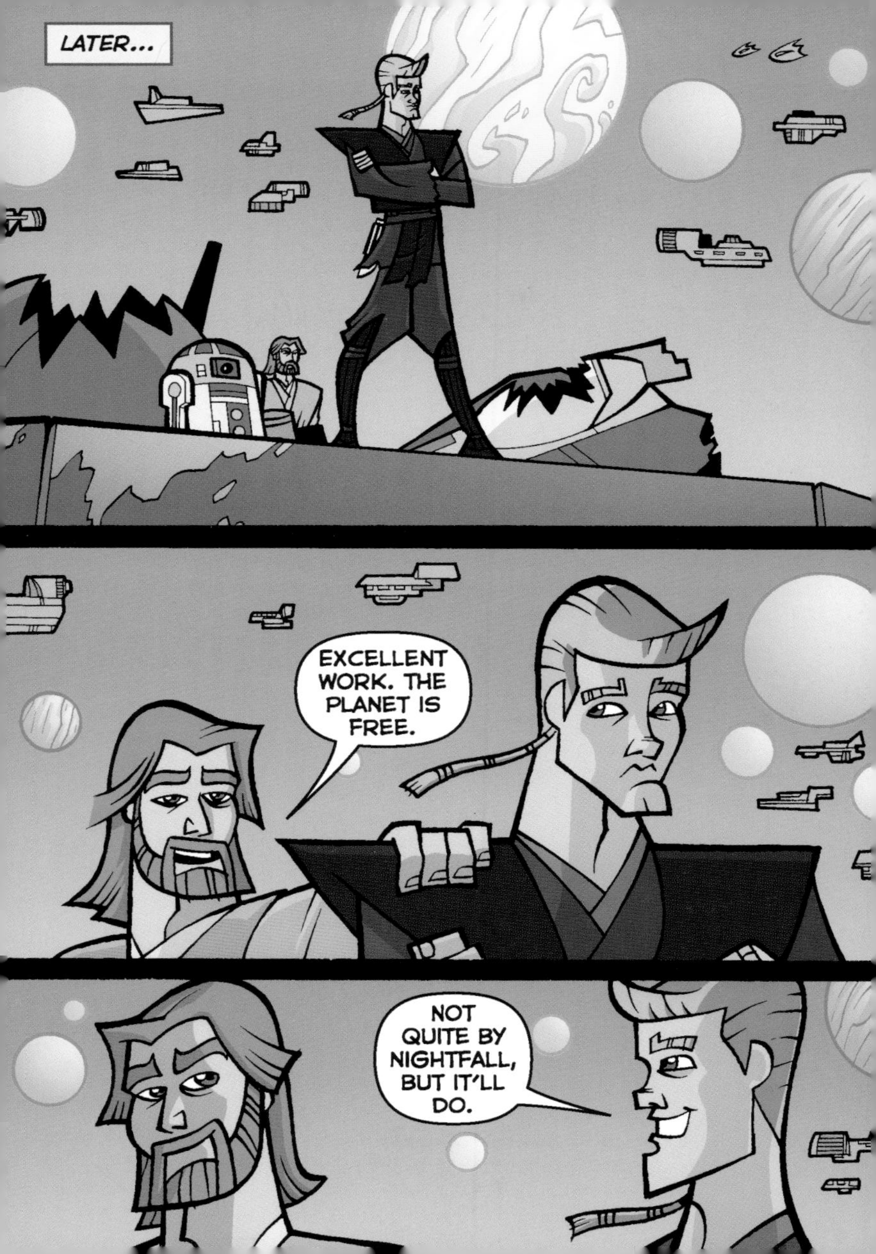
LATER...
EXCELLENT WORK. THE PLANET IS FREE.
NOT QUITE BY NIGHTFALL, BUT IT'LL DO.

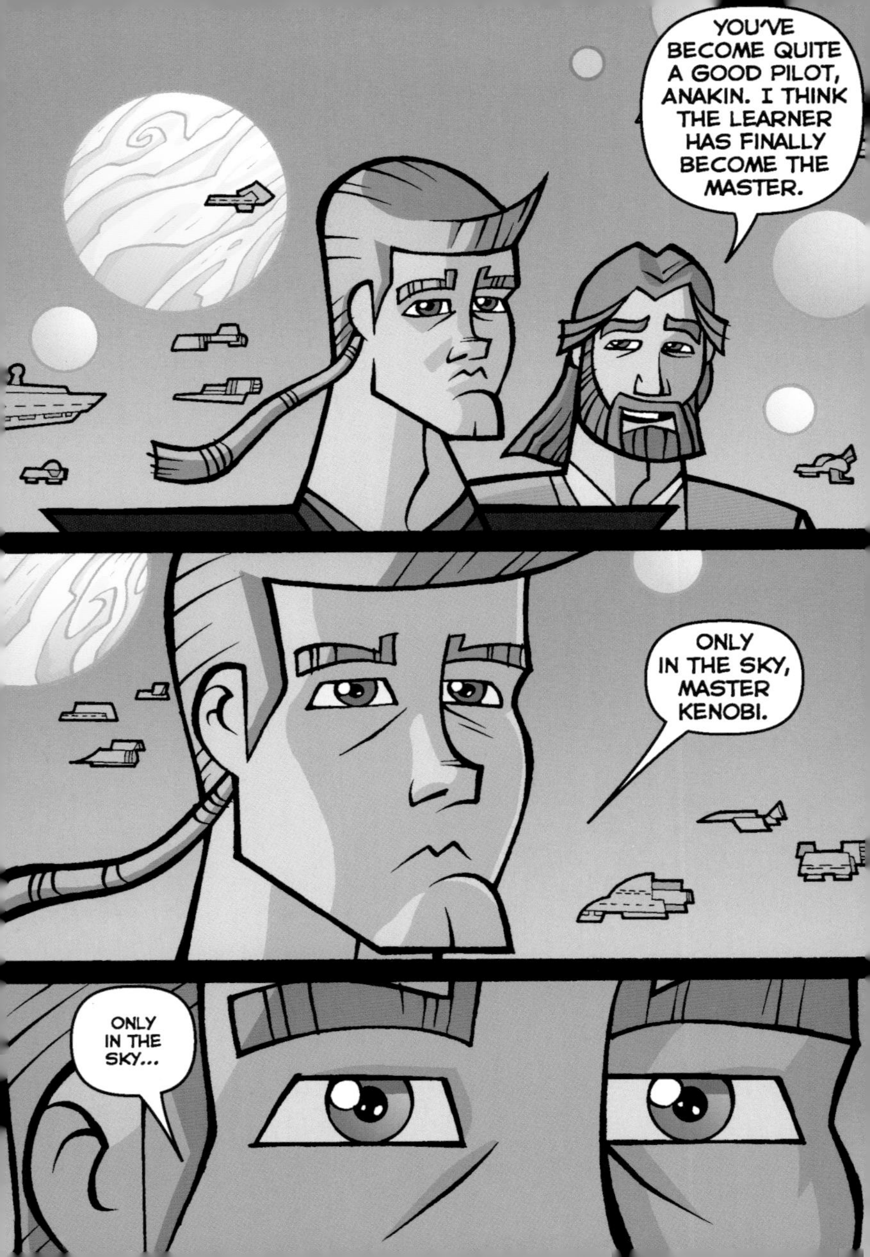
YOU'VE BECOME QUITE A GOOD PILOT, ANAKIN. I THINK THE LEARNER HAS FINALLY BECOME THE MASTER.
ONLY IN THE SKY, MASTER KENOBI.
ONLY IN THE SKY...

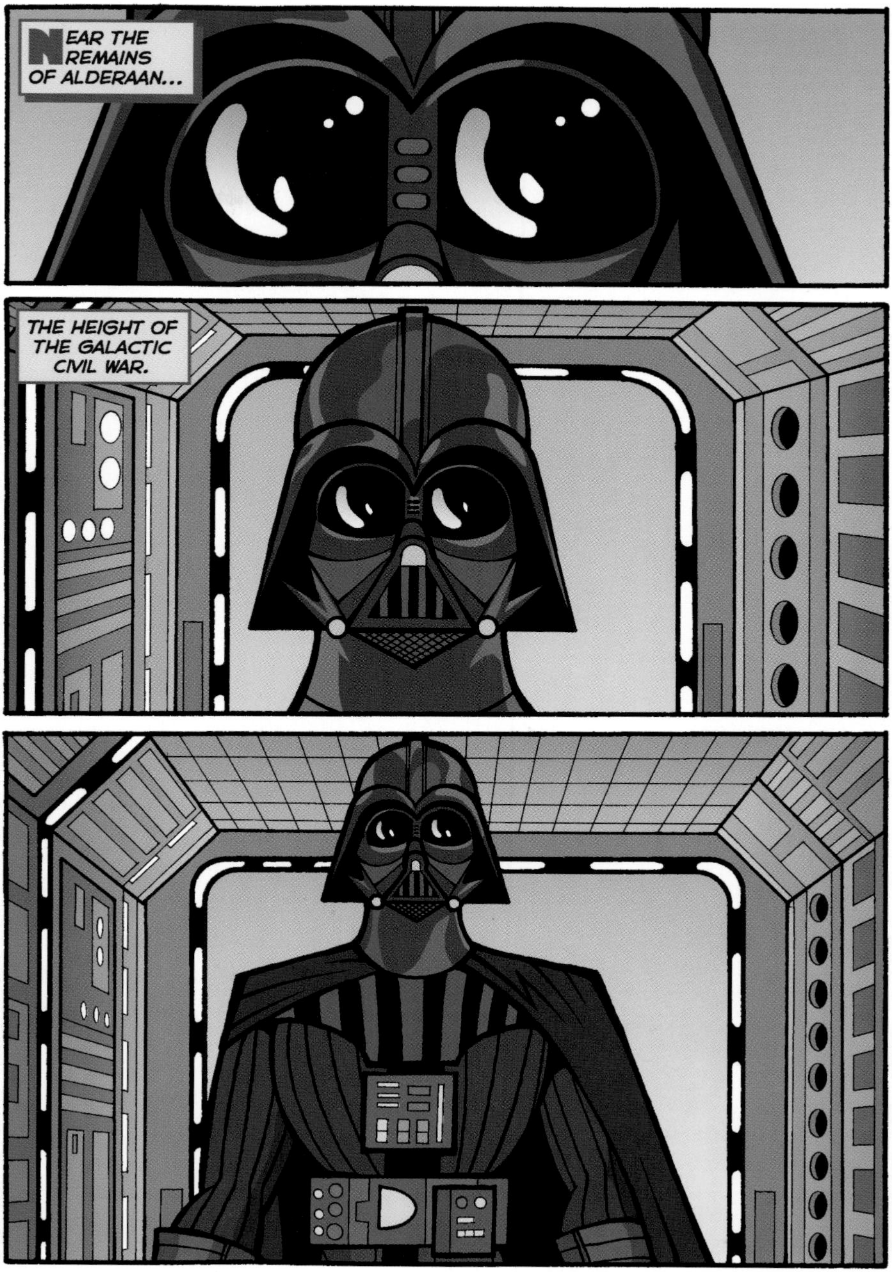
NEAR THE REMAINS OF ALDERAAN...
THE HEIGHT OF THE GALACTIC CIVIL WAR.

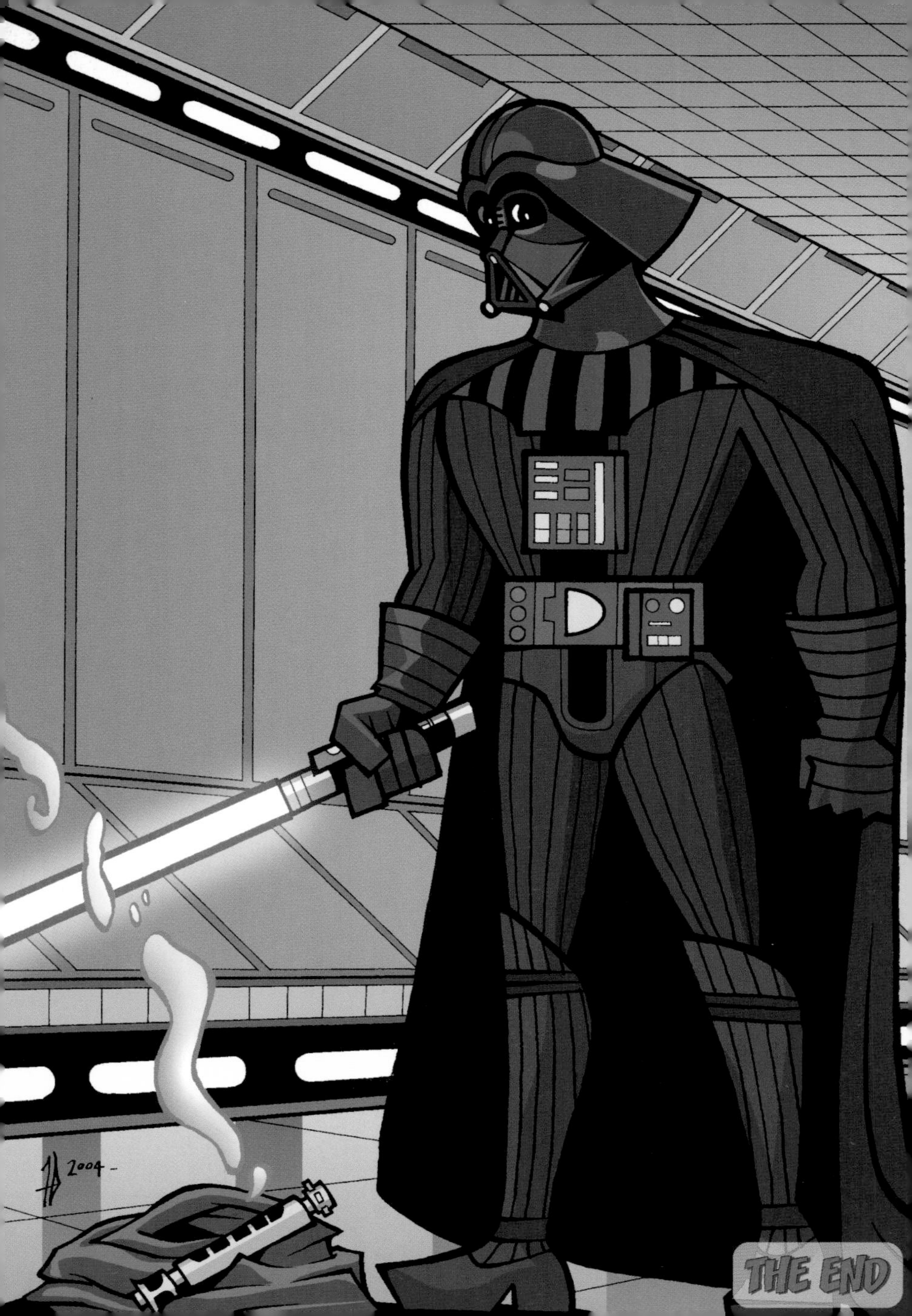
2004
THE END

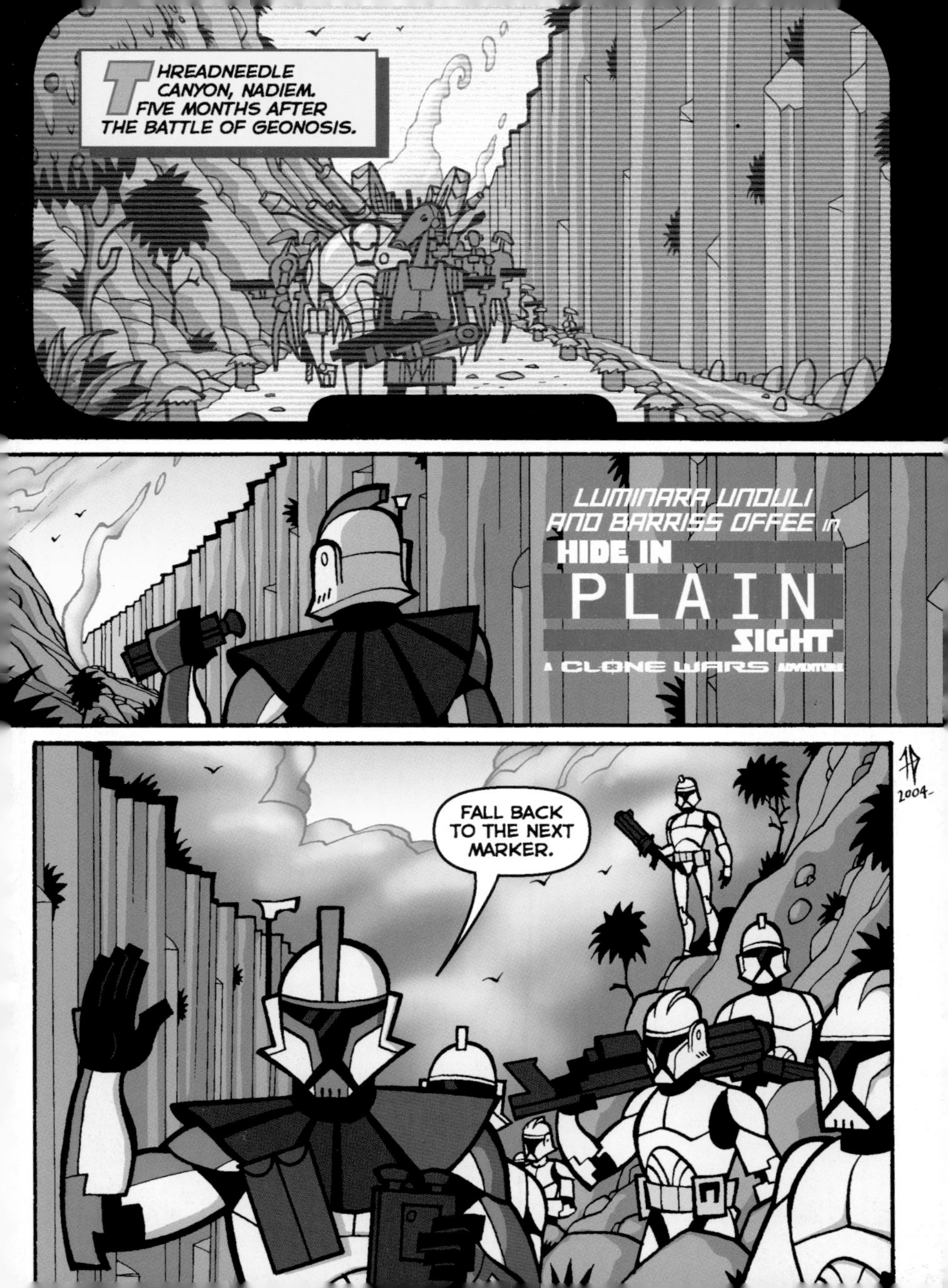
THREADNEEDLE CANYON, NADIEM. FIVE MONTHS AFTER THE BATTLE OF GEONOSIS.
LUMINARA UNDULI AND BARRISS OFFEE in
HIDE IN PLAIN SIGHT
A CLONE WARS ADVENTURE
FALL BACK TO THE NEXT MARKER.
2004

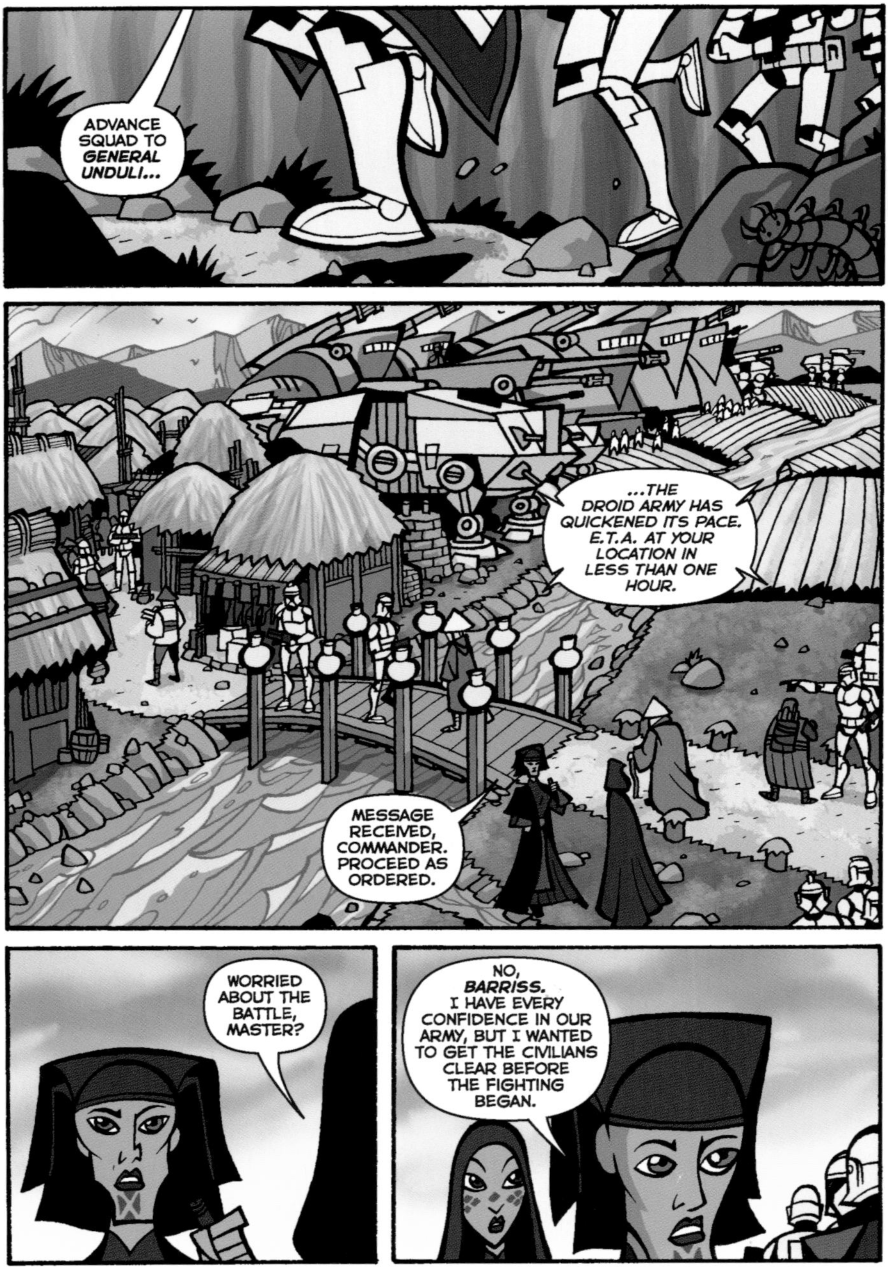
ADVANCE SQUAD TO GENERAL UNDULI...
...THE DROID ARMY HAS QUICKENED ITS PACE. E.T.A. AT YOUR LOCATION IN LESS THAN ONE HOUR.
MESSAGE RECEIVED, COMMANDER. PROCEED AS ORDERED.
WORRIED ABOUT THE BATTLE, MASTER?
NO, BARRISS. I HAVE EVERY CONFIDENCE IN OUR ARMY, BUT I WANTED TO GET THE CIVILIANS CLEAR BEFORE THE FIGHTING BEGAN.

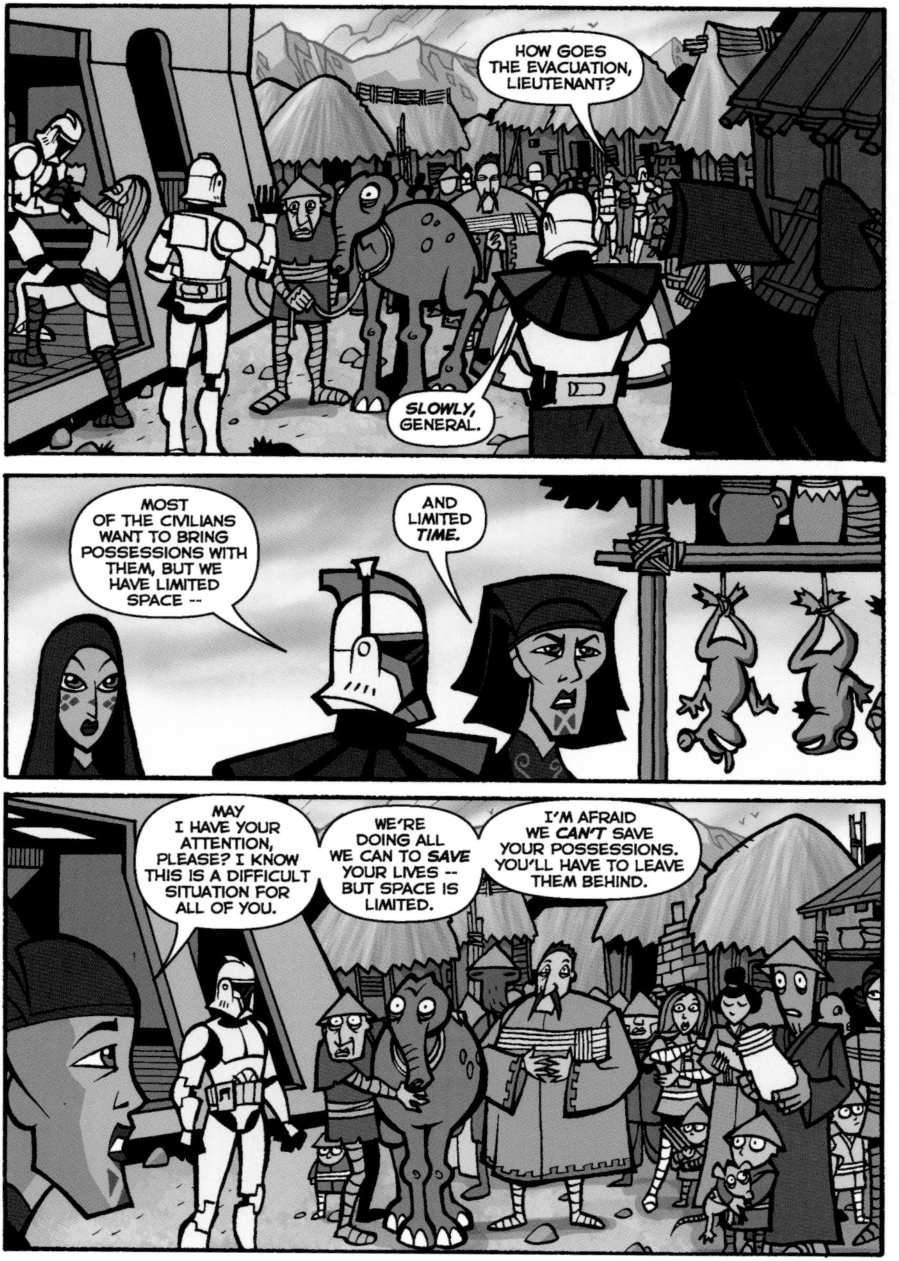
HOW GOES THE EVACUATION, LIEUTENANT?
SLOWLY, GENERAL.
MOST OF THE CIVILIANS WANT TO BRING POSSESSIONS WITH THEM, BUT WE HAVE LIMITED SPACE --
AND LIMITED TIME.
MAY I HAVE YOUR ATTENTION, PLEASE? I KNOW THIS IS A DIFFICULT SITUATION FOR ALL OF YOU.
WE'RE DOING ALL WE CAN TO SAVE YOUR LIVES -- BUT SPACE IS LIMITED.
I'M AFRAID WE CAN'T SAVE YOUR POSSESSIONS. YOU'LL HAVE TO LEAVE THEM BEHIND.

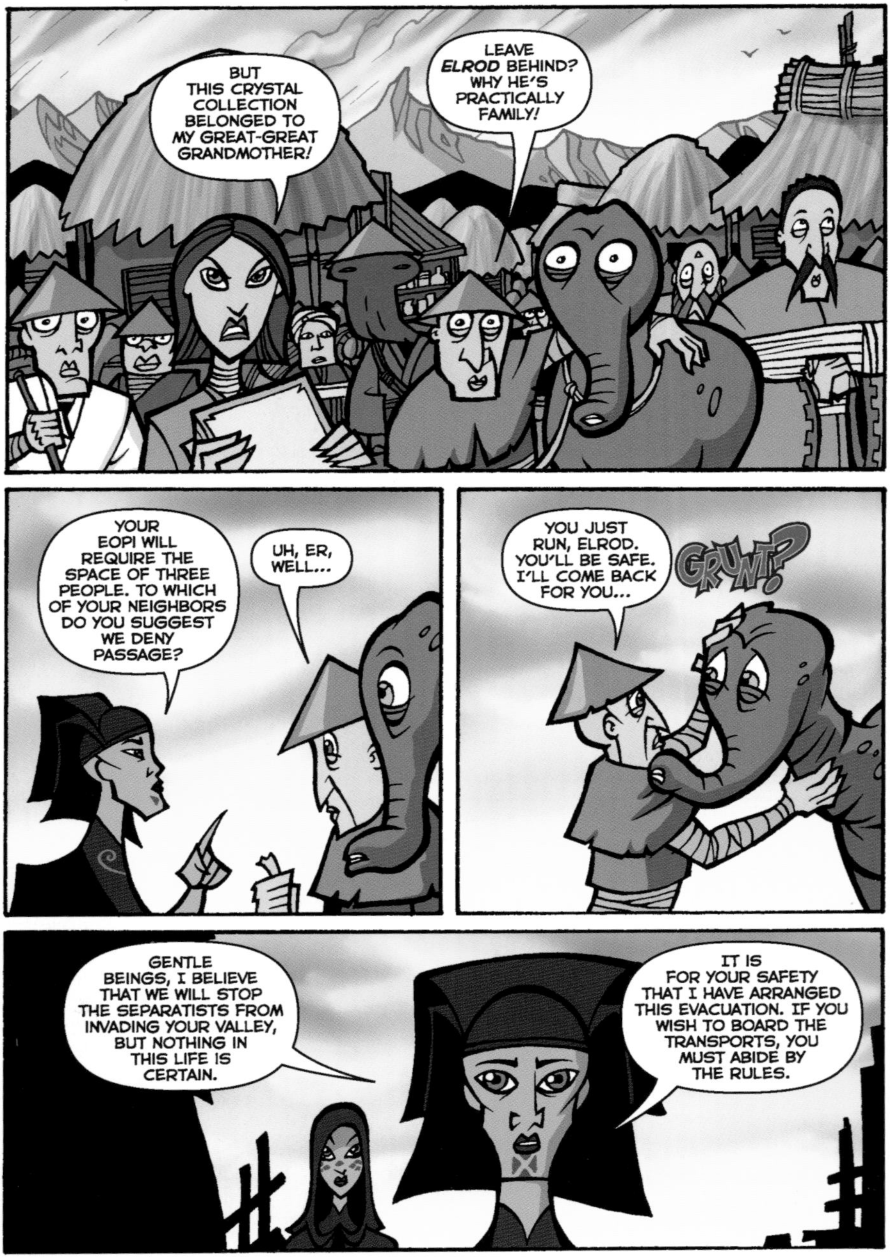
BUT THIS CRYSTAL COLLECTION BELONGED TO MY GREAT-GREAT GRANDMOTHER!
LEAVE *ELROD* BEHIND? WHY HE'S PRACTICALLY FAMILY!
YOUR EOPI WILL REQUIRE THE SPACE OF THREE PEOPLE. TO WHICH OF YOUR NEIGHBORS DO YOU SUGGEST WE DENY PASSAGE?
UH, ER, WELL...
YOU JUST RUN, ELROD. YOU'LL BE SAFE. I'LL COME BACK FOR YOU...
GRUNT?
GENTLE BEINGS, I BELIEVE THAT WE WILL STOP THE SEPARATISTS FROM INVADING YOUR VALLEY, BUT NOTHING IN THIS LIFE IS CERTAIN.
IT IS FOR YOUR SAFETY THAT I HAVE ARRANGED THIS EVACUATION. IF YOU WISH TO BOARD THE TRANSPORTS, YOU MUST ABIDE BY THE RULES.

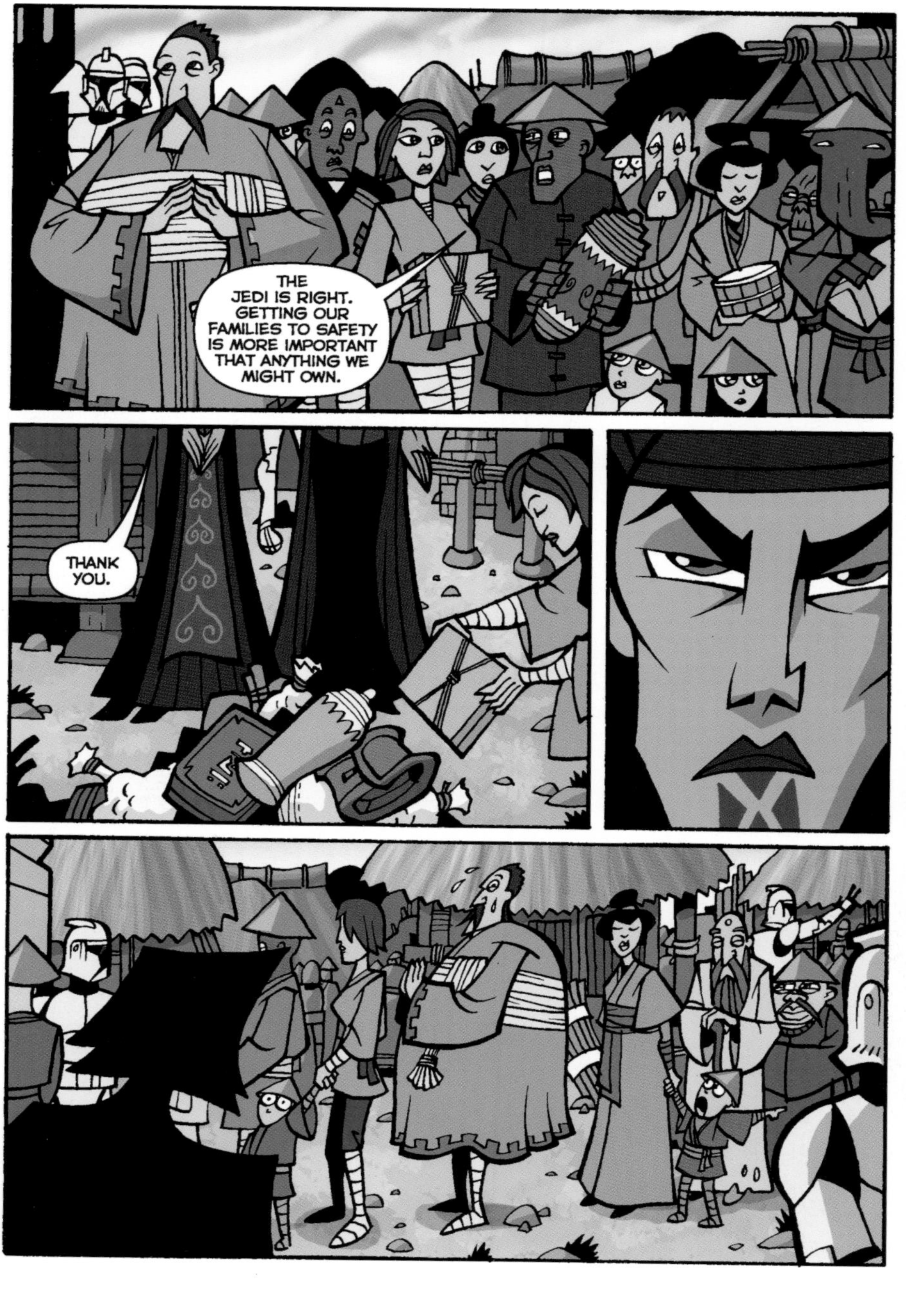
THE JEDI IS RIGHT. GETTING OUR FAMILIES TO SAFETY IS MORE IMPORTANT THAT ANYTHING WE MIGHT OWN.
THANK YOU.

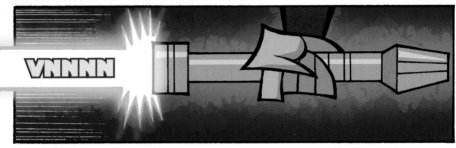

VNNNN

NO!

SWIIIK!

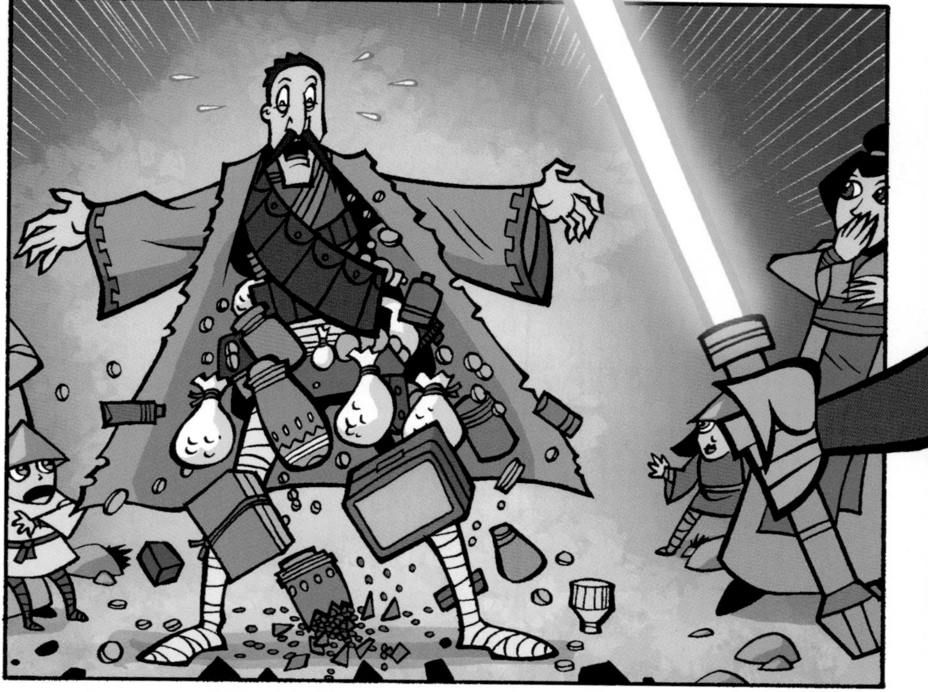

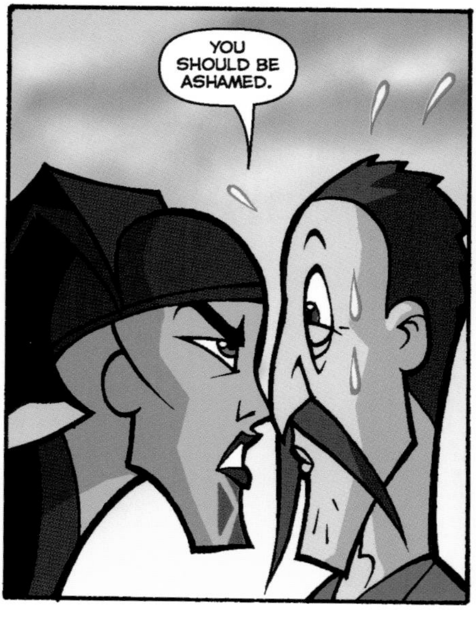
YOU SHOULD BE ASHAMED.

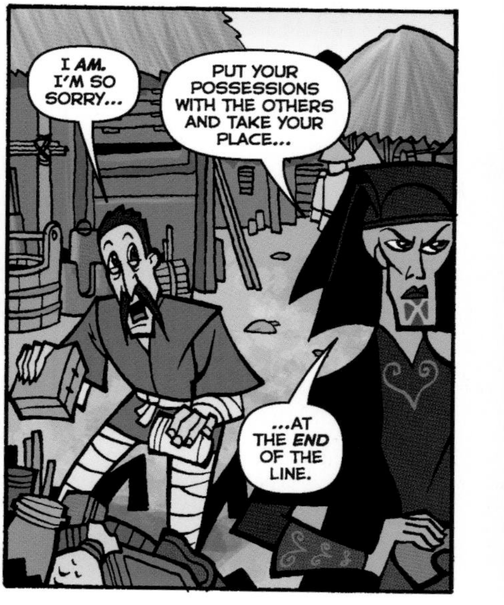
I *AM.* I'M SO SORRY...
PUT YOUR POSSESSIONS WITH THE OTHERS AND TAKE YOUR PLACE...
...AT THE *END* OF THE LINE.

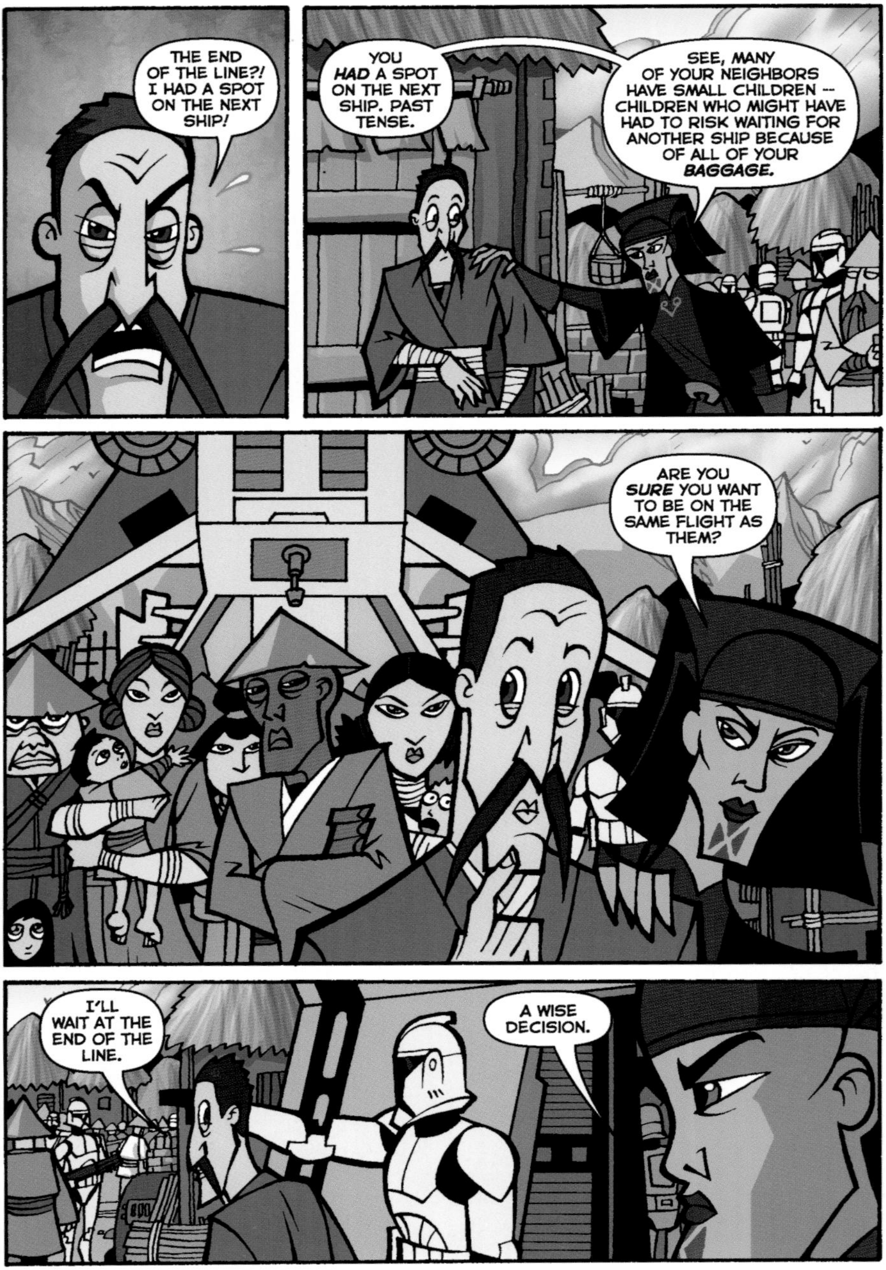
THE END OF THE LINE?! I HAD A SPOT ON THE NEXT SHIP!
YOU HAD A SPOT ON THE NEXT SHIP. PAST TENSE.
SEE, MANY OF YOUR NEIGHBORS HAVE SMALL CHILDREN -- CHILDREN WHO MIGHT HAVE HAD TO RISK WAITING FOR ANOTHER SHIP BECAUSE OF ALL OF YOUR BAGGAGE.
ARE YOU SURE YOU WANT TO BE ON THE SAME FLIGHT AS THEM?
I'LL WAIT AT THE END OF THE LINE.
A WISE DECISION.

HOW DID YOU KNOW HE WAS HIDING SOMETHING?

BECAUSE HE WAS THE *ONLY* PERSON IN LINE *NOT* CARRYING SOMETHING.

SOMETIMES TRYING TOO HARD TO ESCAPE DETECTION WILL DRAW ATTENTION TO ONE'S SELF.

BESIDES, FOR A MAN OF HIS APPARENT GIRTH, HE HAD AWFULLY SKINNY LEGS!

GENERAL -- !

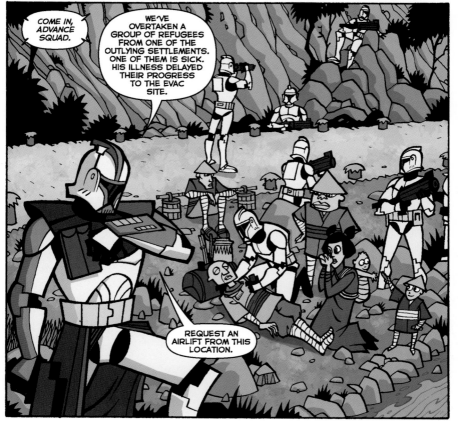

COME IN, ADVANCE SQUAD.

WE'VE OVERTAKEN A GROUP OF REFUGEES FROM ONE OF THE OUTLYING SETTLEMENTS. ONE OF THEM IS SICK. HIS ILLNESS DELAYED THEIR PROGRESS TO THE EVAC SITE.

REQUEST AN AIRLIFT FROM THIS LOCATION.

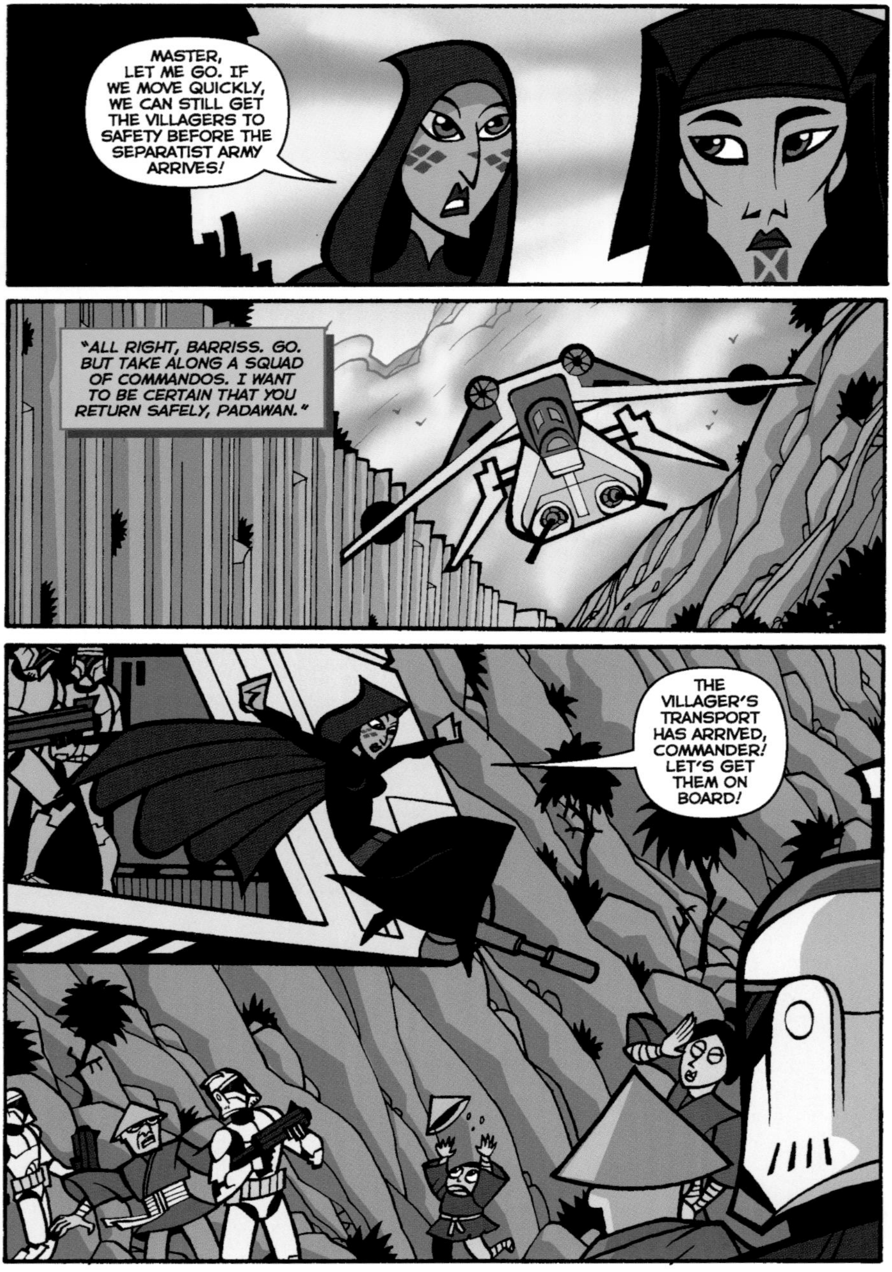
MASTER, LET ME GO. IF WE MOVE QUICKLY, WE CAN STILL GET THE VILLAGERS TO SAFETY BEFORE THE SEPARATIST ARMY ARRIVES!
"ALL RIGHT, BARRISS. GO. BUT TAKE ALONG A SQUAD OF COMMANDOS. I WANT TO BE CERTAIN THAT YOU RETURN SAFELY, PADAWAN."
THE VILLAGER'S TRANSPORT HAS ARRIVED, COMMANDER! LET'S GET THEM ON BOARD!

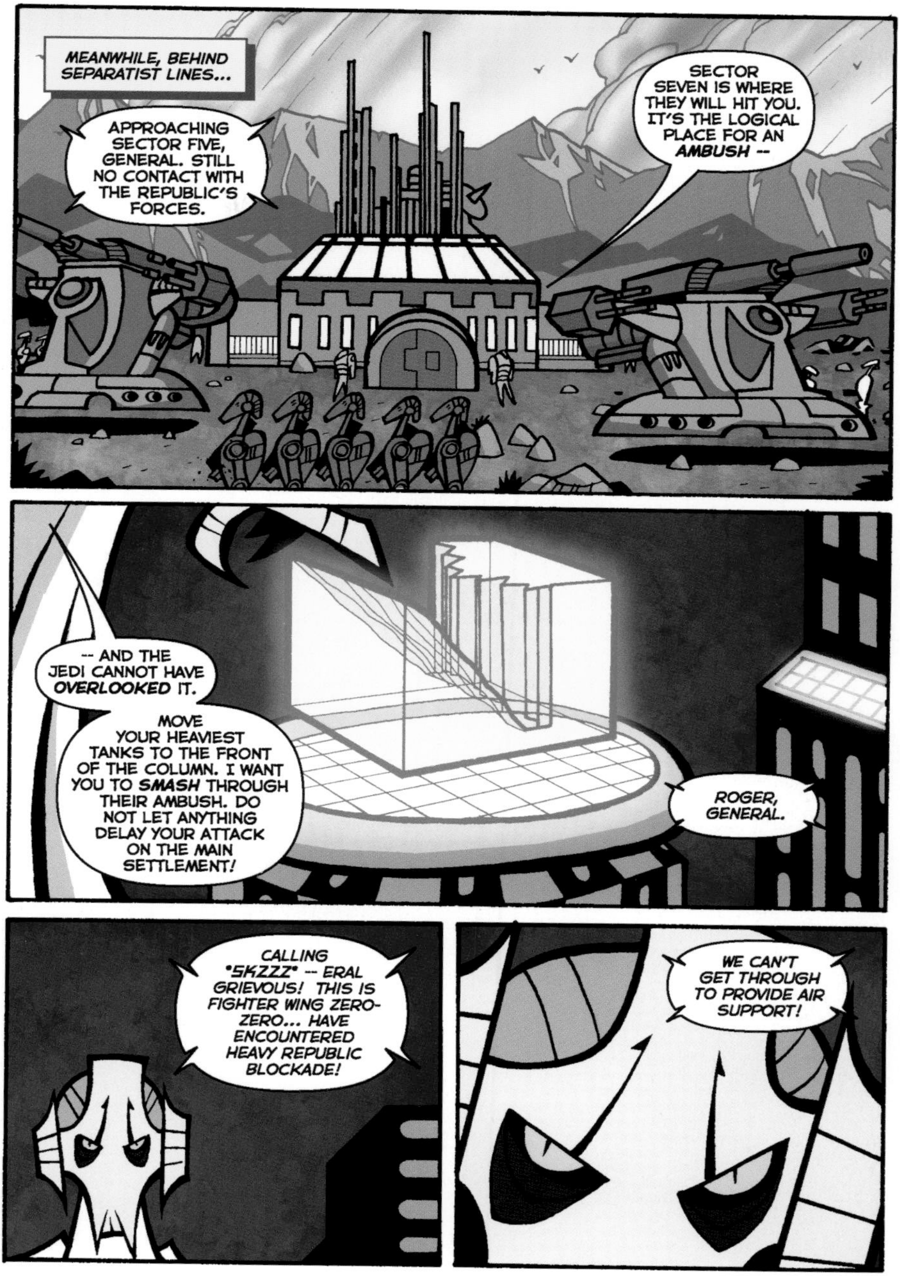
MEANWHILE, BEHIND SEPARATIST LINES...
APPROACHING SECTOR FIVE, GENERAL. STILL NO CONTACT WITH THE REPUBLIC'S FORCES.
SECTOR SEVEN IS WHERE THEY WILL HIT YOU. IT'S THE LOGICAL PLACE FOR AN AMBUSH --
-- AND THE JEDI CANNOT HAVE OVERLOOKED IT.
MOVE YOUR HEAVIEST TANKS TO THE FRONT OF THE COLUMN. I WANT YOU TO SMASH THROUGH THEIR AMBUSH. DO NOT LET ANYTHING DELAY YOUR ATTACK ON THE MAIN SETTLEMENT!
ROGER, GENERAL.
CALLING *SKZZZ* -- ERAL GRIEVOUS! THIS IS FIGHTER WING ZERO-ZERO... HAVE ENCOUNTERED HEAVY REPUBLIC BLOCKADE!
WE CAN'T GET THROUGH TO PROVIDE AIR SUPPORT!

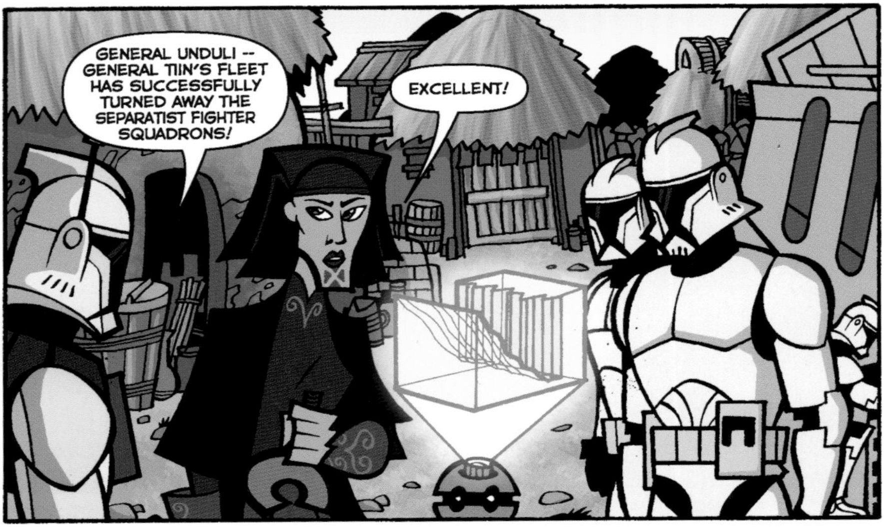
GENERAL UNDULI -- GENERAL TIIN'S FLEET HAS SUCCESSFULLY TURNED AWAY THE SEPARATIST FIGHTER SQUADRONS!
EXCELLENT!

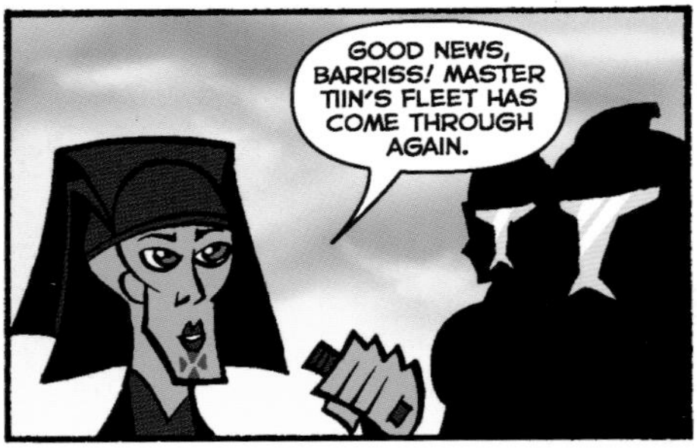
GOOD NEWS, BARRISS! MASTER TIIN'S FLEET HAS COME THROUGH AGAIN.

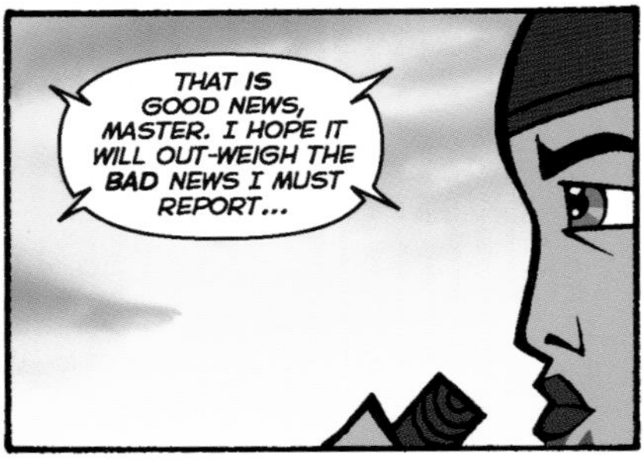
THAT IS GOOD NEWS, MASTER. I HOPE IT WILL OUT-WEIGH THE BAD NEWS I MUST REPORT...

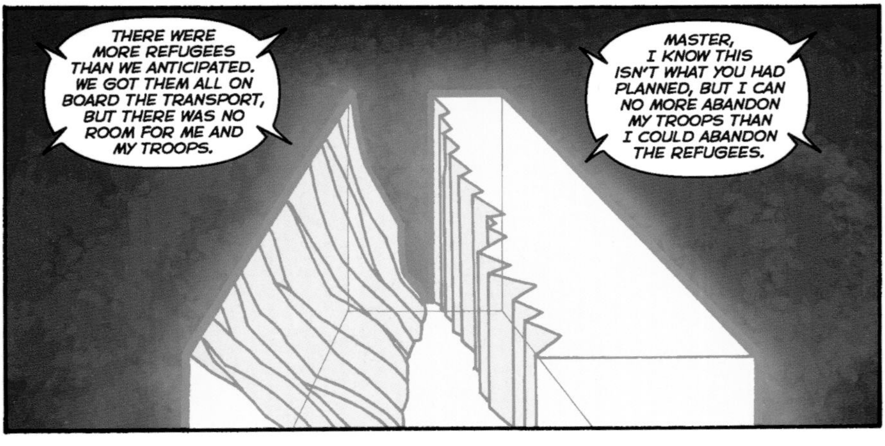
THERE WERE MORE REFUGEES THAN WE ANTICIPATED. WE GOT THEM ALL ON BOARD THE TRANSPORT, BUT THERE WAS NO ROOM FOR ME AND MY TROOPS.
MASTER, I KNOW THIS ISN'T WHAT YOU HAD PLANNED, BUT I CAN NO MORE ABANDON MY TROOPS THAN I COULD ABANDON THE REFUGEES.

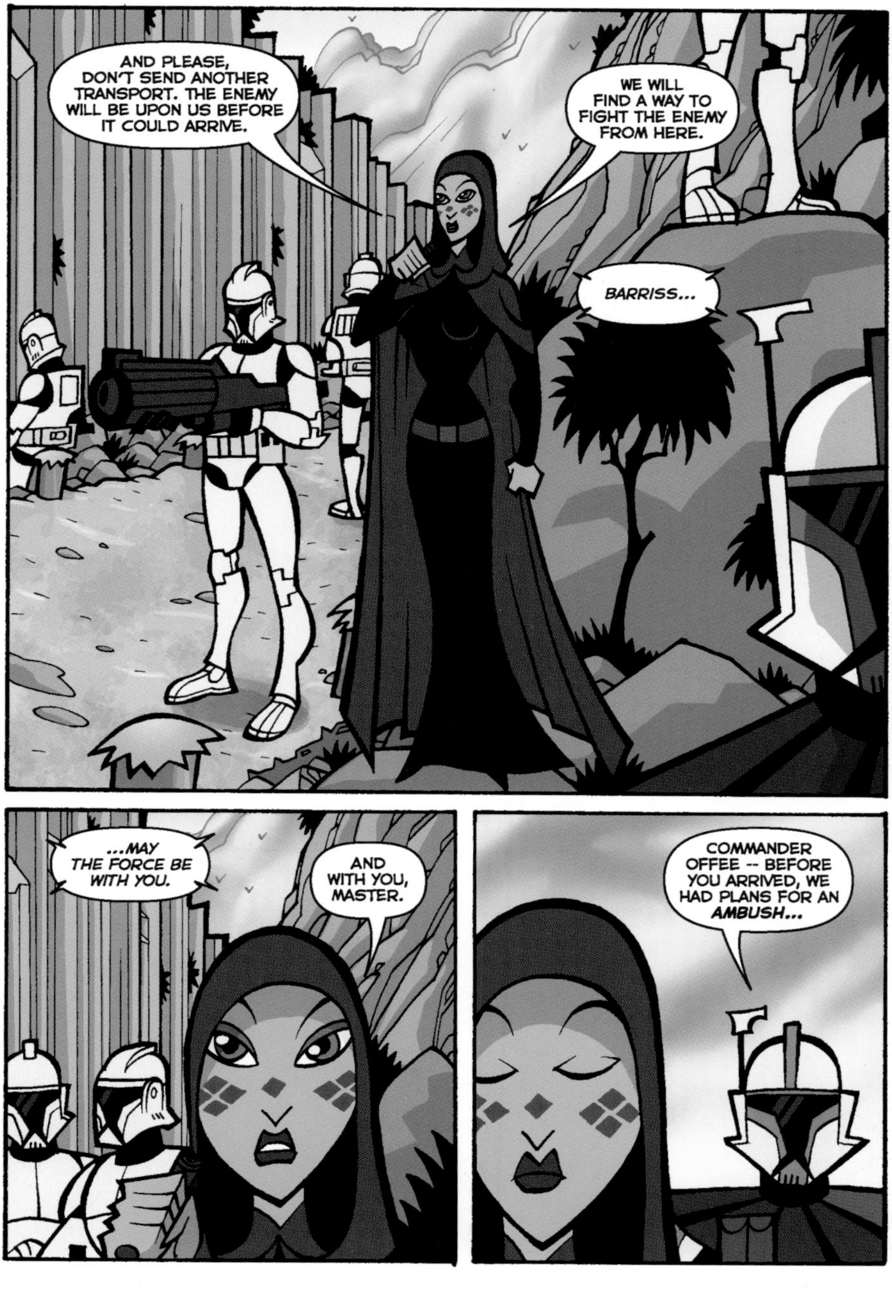
AND PLEASE, DON'T SEND ANOTHER TRANSPORT. THE ENEMY WILL BE UPON US BEFORE IT COULD ARRIVE.
WE WILL FIND A WAY TO FIGHT THE ENEMY FROM HERE.
BARRISS...
...MAY THE FORCE BE WITH YOU.
AND WITH YOU, MASTER.
COMMANDER OFFEE -- BEFORE YOU ARRIVED, WE HAD PLANS FOR AN AMBUSH...

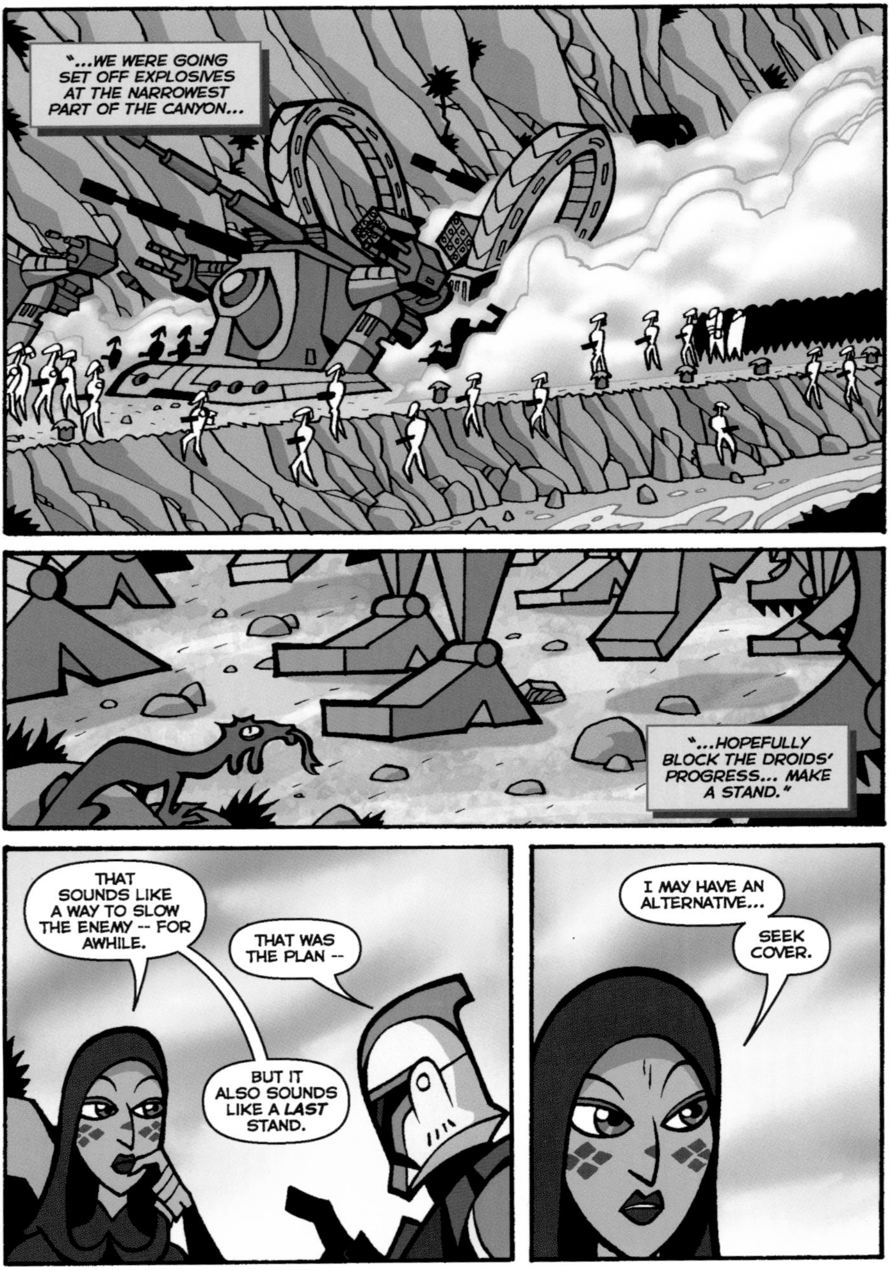
"...WE WERE GOING SET OFF EXPLOSIVES AT THE NARROWEST PART OF THE CANYON...
"...HOPEFULLY BLOCK THE DROIDS' PROGRESS... MAKE A STAND."
THAT SOUNDS LIKE A WAY TO SLOW THE ENEMY -- FOR AWHILE.
THAT WAS THE PLAN --
BUT IT ALSO SOUNDS LIKE A *LAST* STAND.
I MAY HAVE AN ALTERNATIVE...
SEEK COVER.

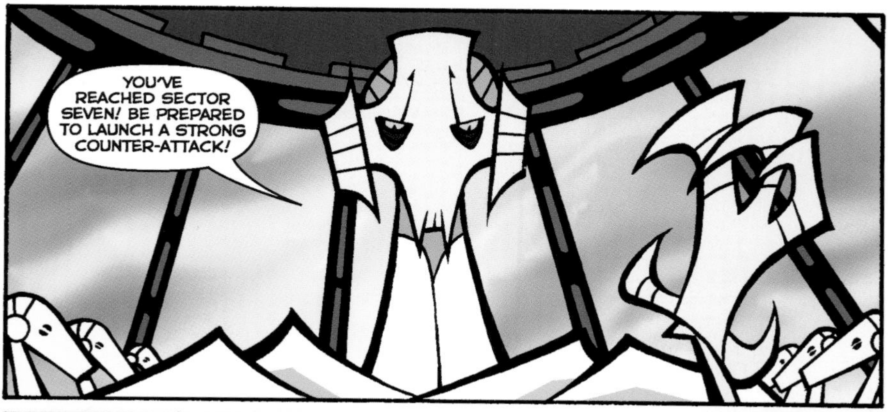
YOU'VE REACHED SECTOR SEVEN! BE PREPARED TO LAUNCH A STRONG COUNTER-ATTACK!

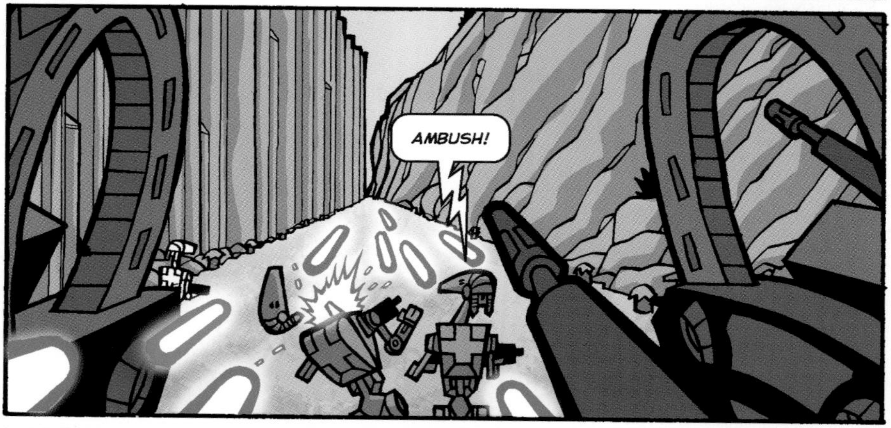
AMBUSH!

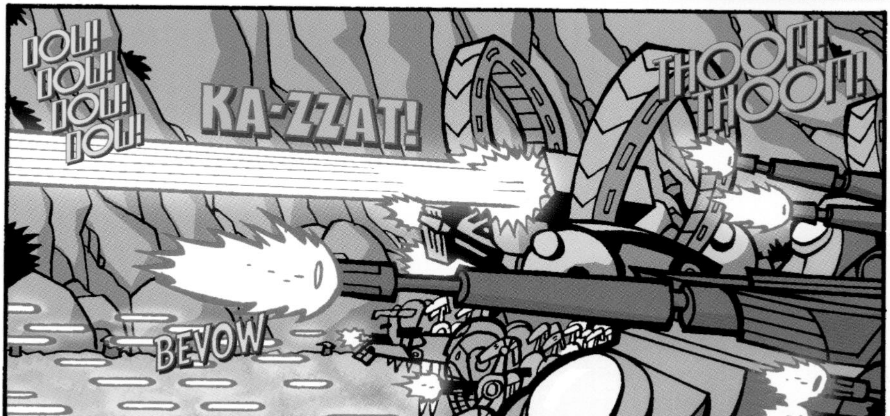
DOW! DOW! DOW! DOW!
KA-ZZAT!
THOOM! THOOM!
BEVOW

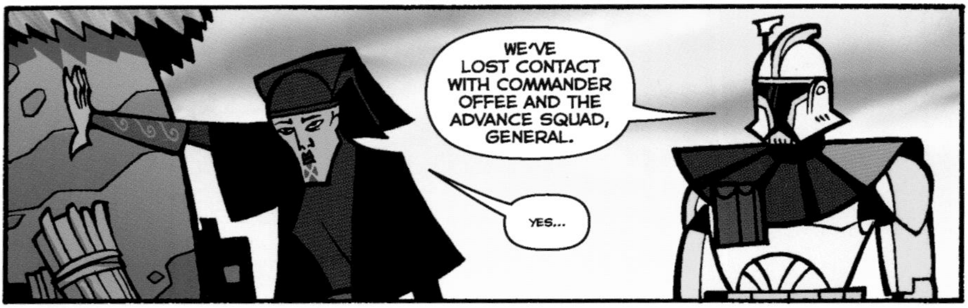
WE'VE LOST CONTACT WITH COMMANDER OFFEE AND THE ADVANCE SQUAD, GENERAL.
YES...

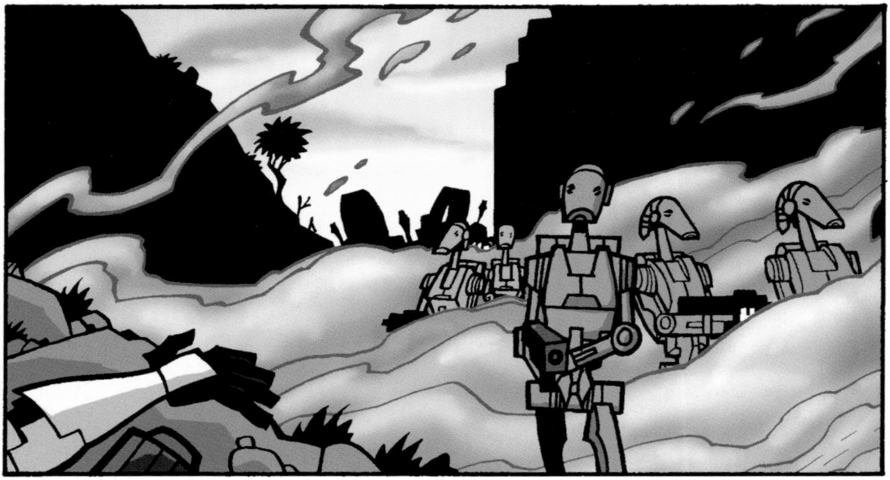

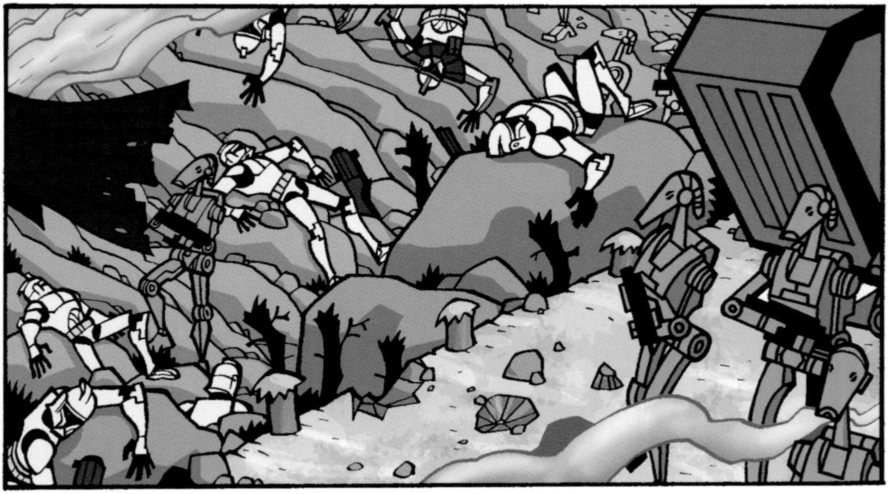

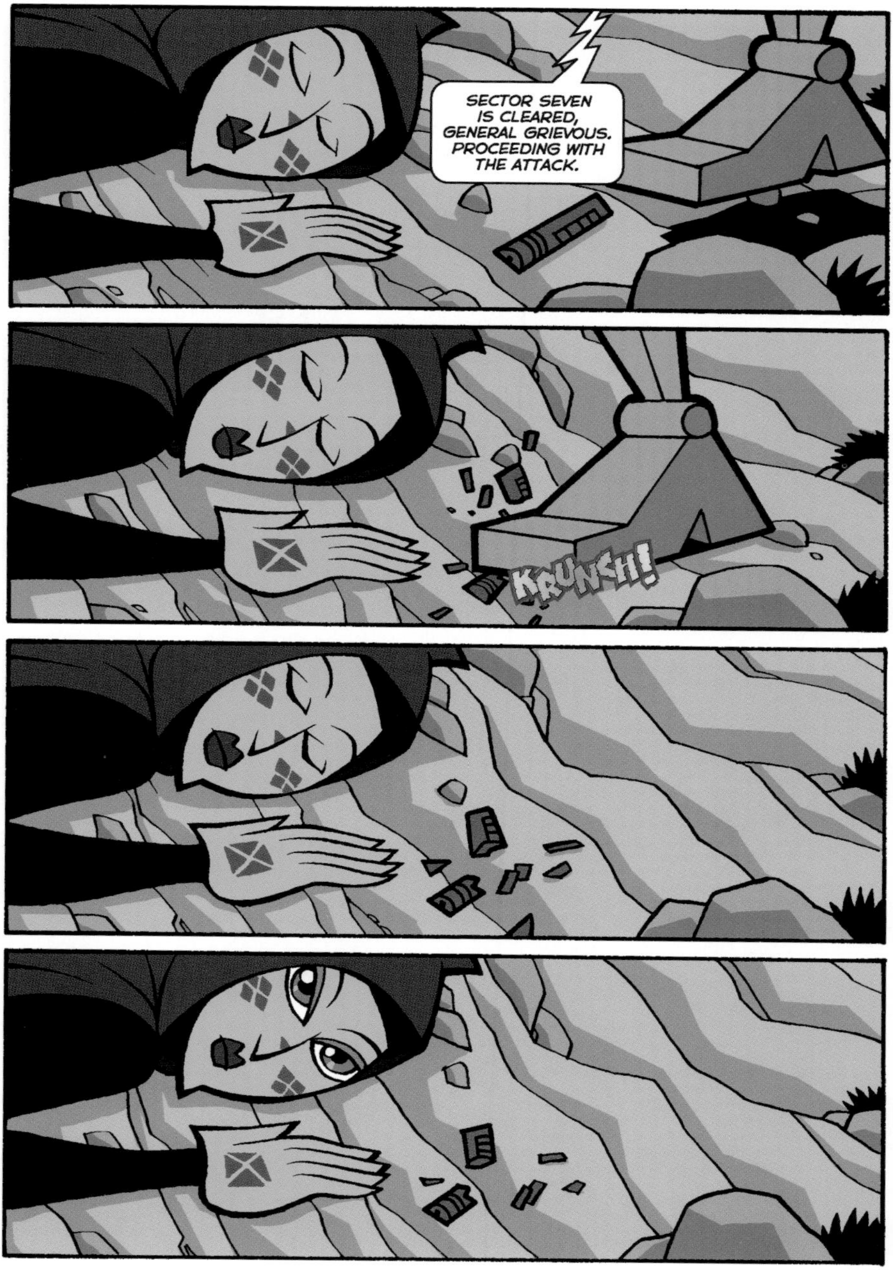
SECTOR SEVEN IS CLEARED, GENERAL GRIEVOUS. PROCEEDING WITH THE ATTACK.
KRUNCH!

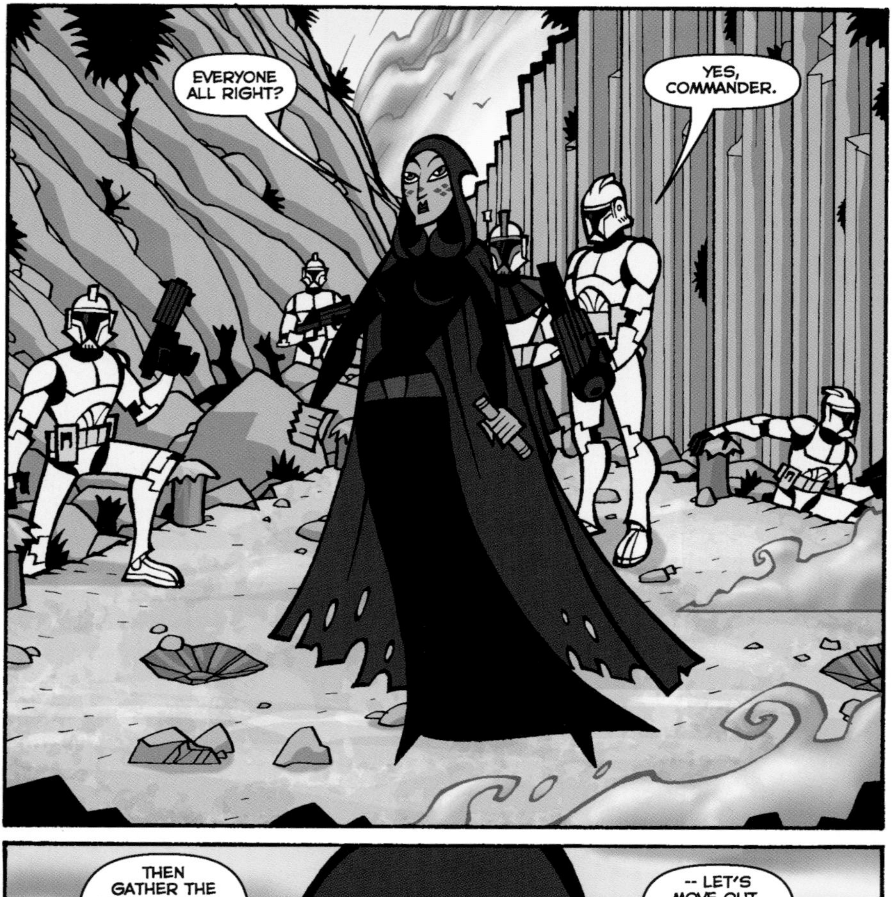
EVERYONE ALL RIGHT?
YES, COMMANDER.

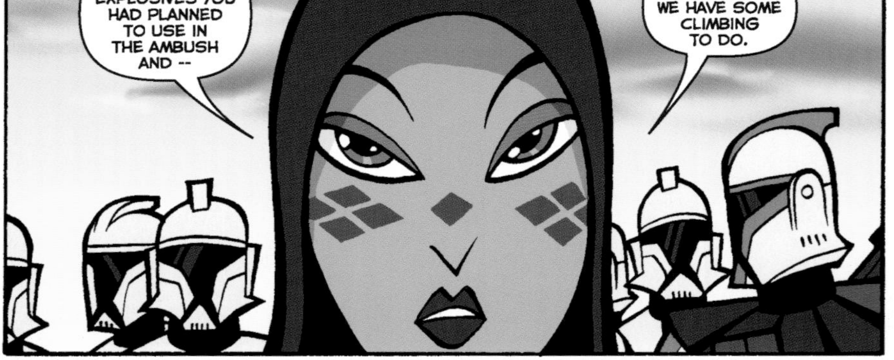
THEN GATHER THE EXPLOSIVES YOU HAD PLANNED TO USE IN THE AMBUSH AND --
-- LET'S MOVE OUT. WE HAVE SOME CLIMBING TO DO.

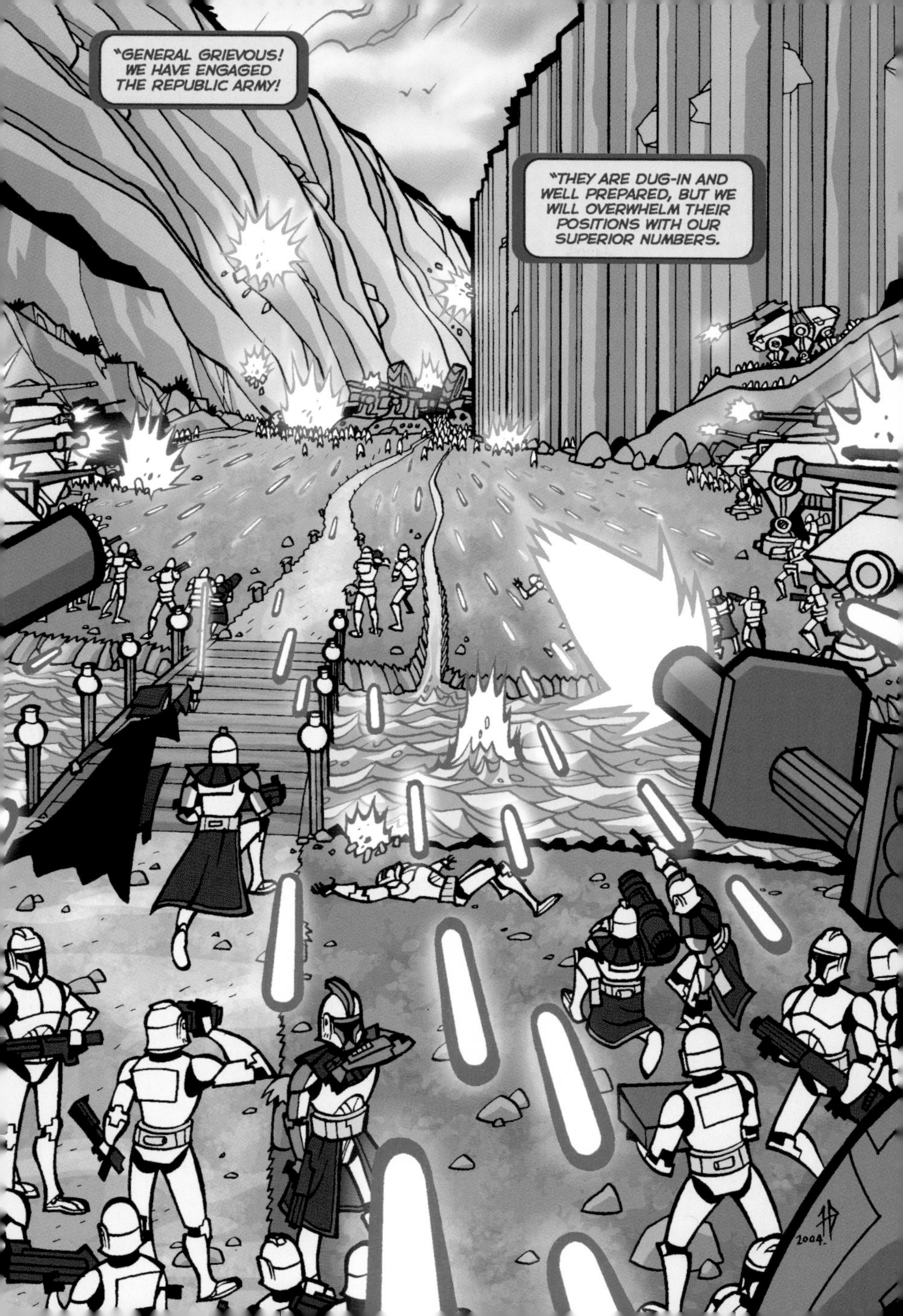
"GENERAL GRIEVOUS! WE HAVE ENGAGED THE REPUBLIC ARMY!
"THEY ARE DUG-IN AND WELL PREPARED, BUT WE WILL OVERWHELM THEIR POSITIONS WITH OUR SUPERIOR NUMBERS.
2004.

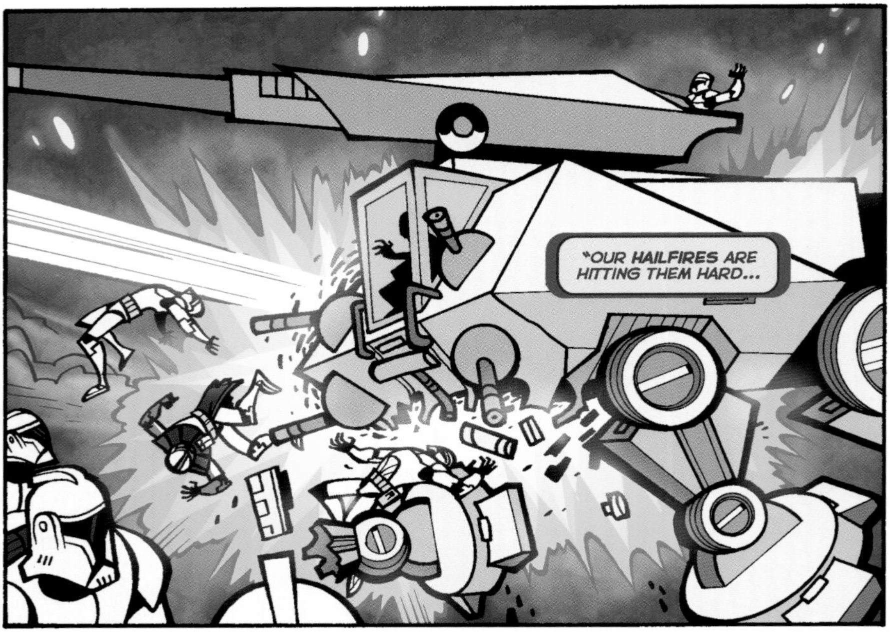
"OUR HAILFIRES ARE HITTING THEM HARD...
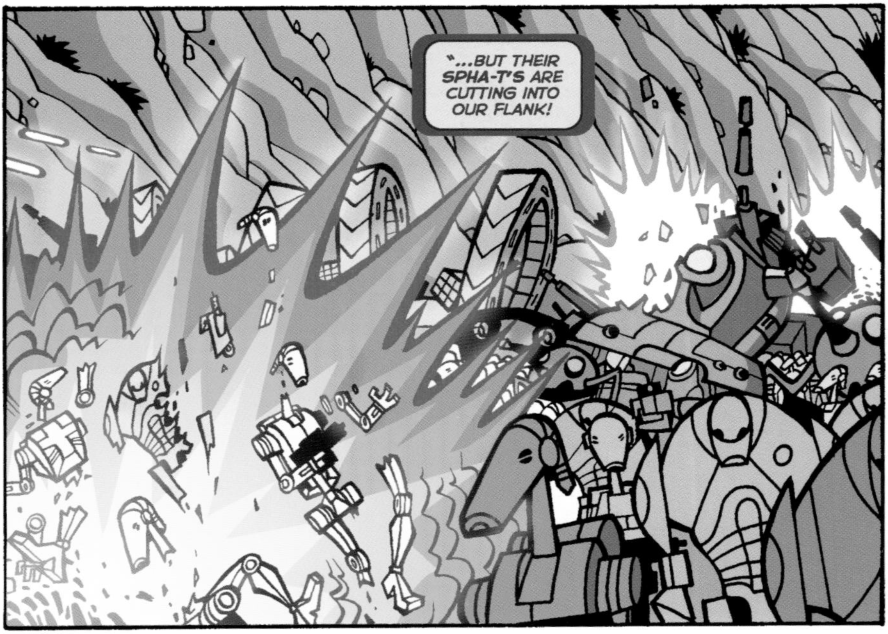
"...BUT THEIR SPHA-T'S ARE CUTTING INTO OUR FLANK!

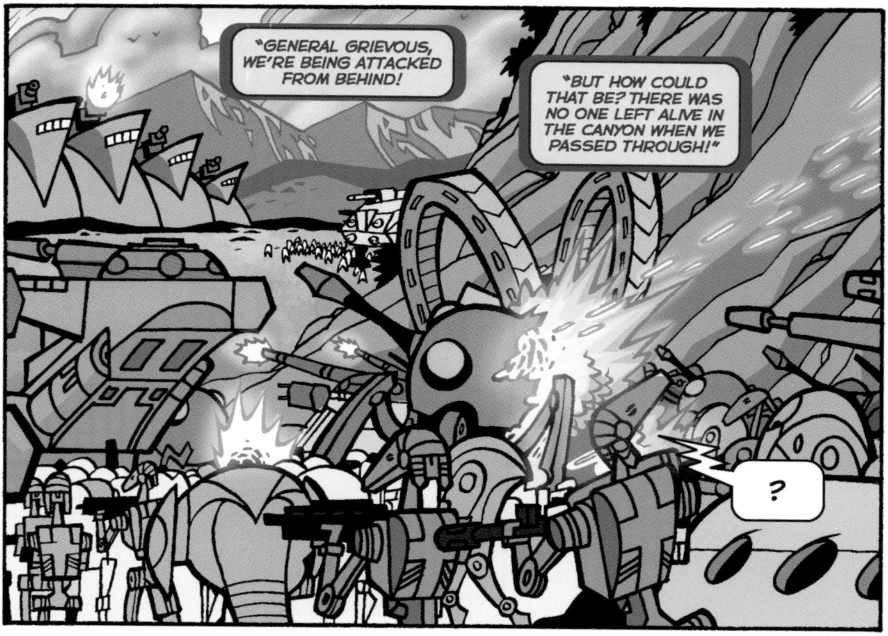
"GENERAL GRIEVOUS, WE'RE BEING ATTACKED FROM BEHIND!
"BUT HOW COULD THAT BE? THERE WAS NO ONE LEFT ALIVE IN THE CANYON WHEN WE PASSED THROUGH!"
?
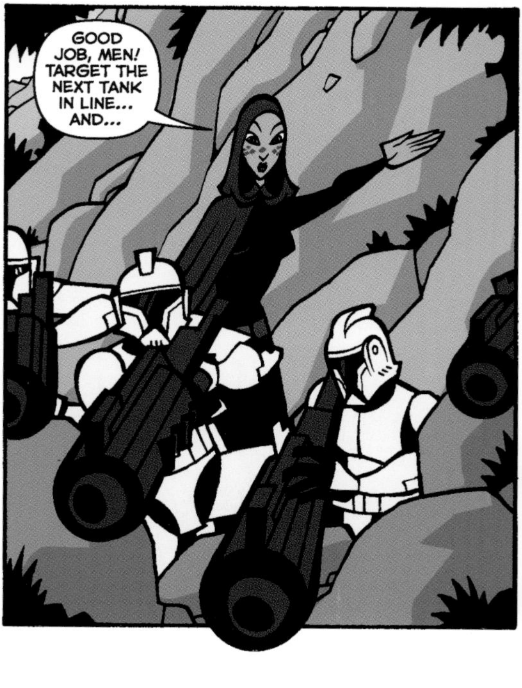
GOOD JOB, MEN! TARGET THE NEXT TANK IN LINE... AND...
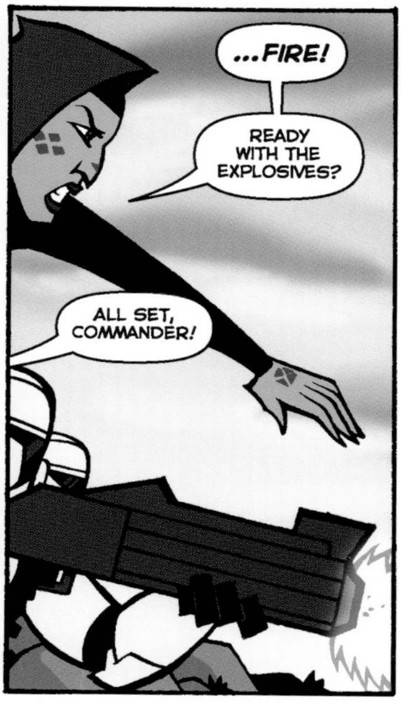
...FIRE!
READY WITH THE EXPLOSIVES?
ALL SET, COMMANDER!

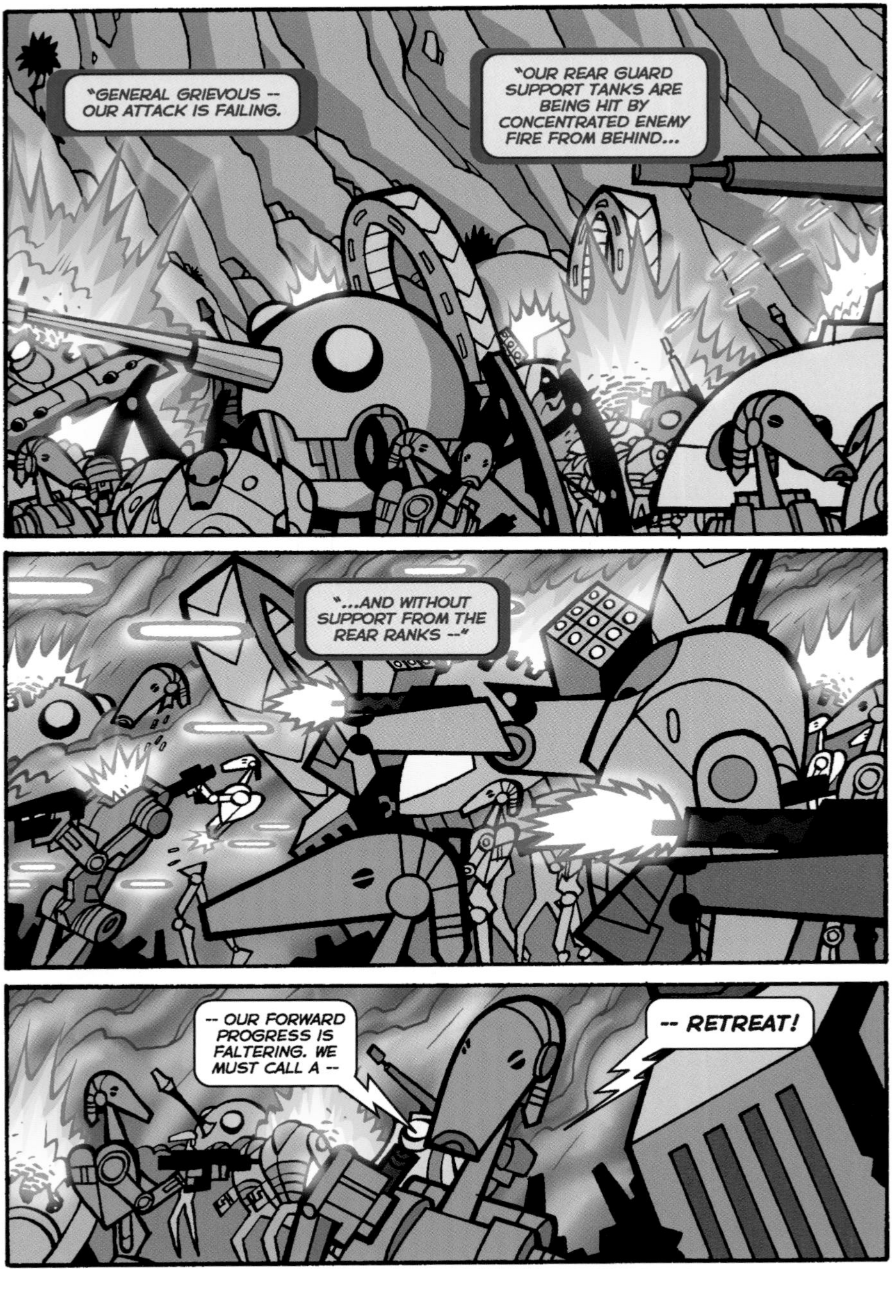
"GENERAL GRIEVOUS -- OUR ATTACK IS FAILING.
"OUR REAR GUARD SUPPORT TANKS ARE BEING HIT BY CONCENTRATED ENEMY FIRE FROM BEHIND...
"...AND WITHOUT SUPPORT FROM THE REAR RANKS --"
-- OUR FORWARD PROGRESS IS FALTERING. WE MUST CALL A --
-- RETREAT!

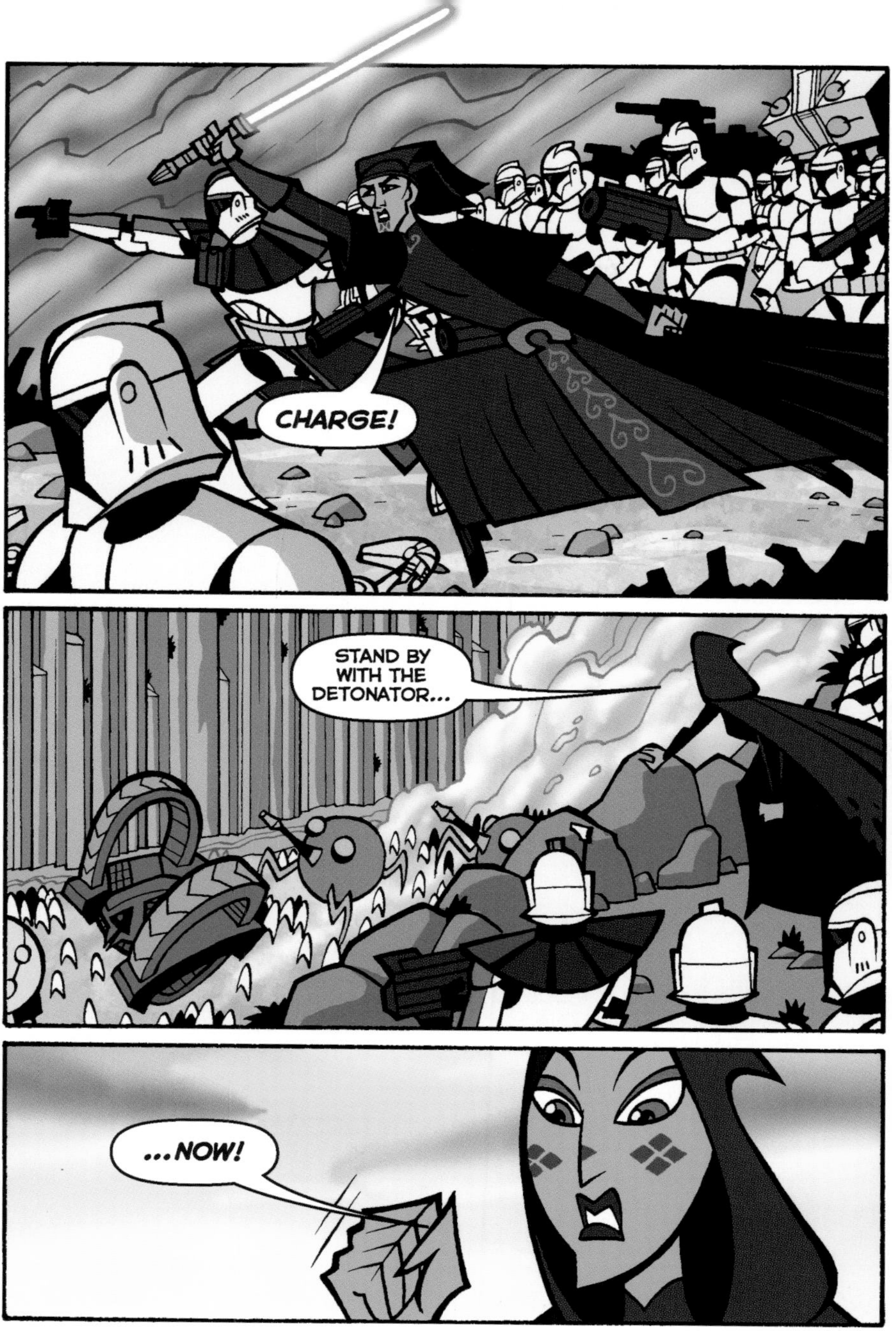
CHARGE!
STAND BY WITH THE DETONATOR...
...NOW!

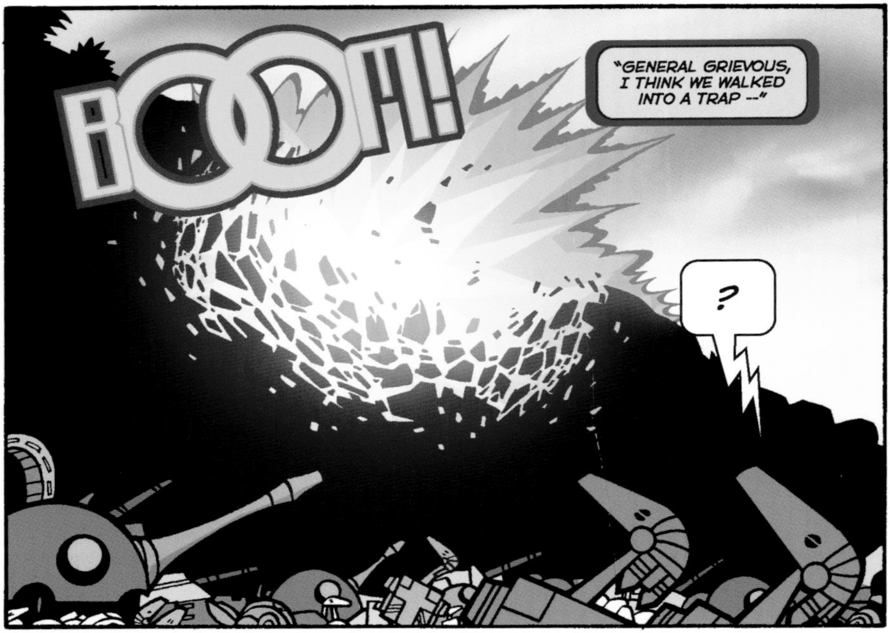
BOOM!
"GENERAL GRIEVOUS, I THINK WE WALKED INTO A TRAP --"
?

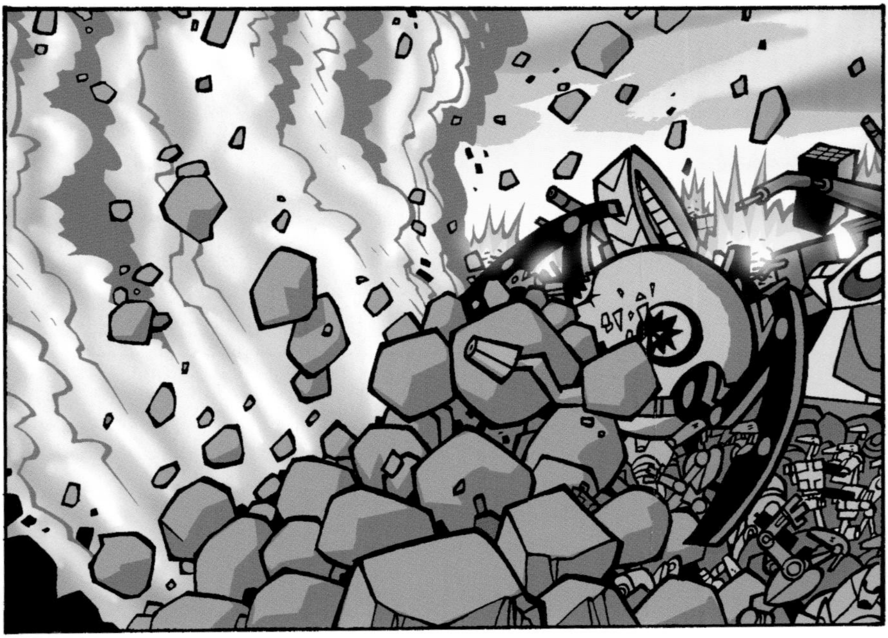

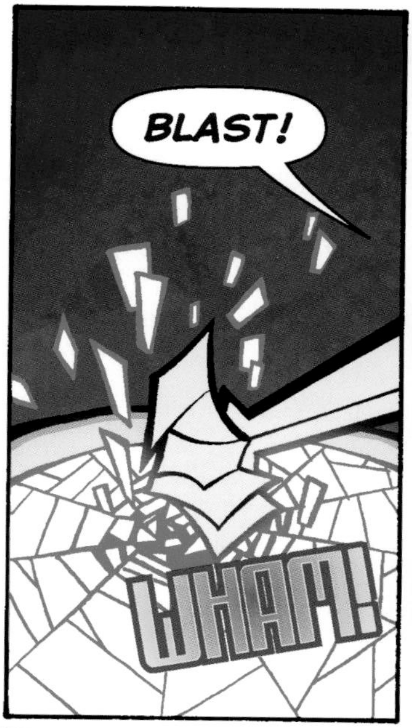
BLAST!
WHAM!
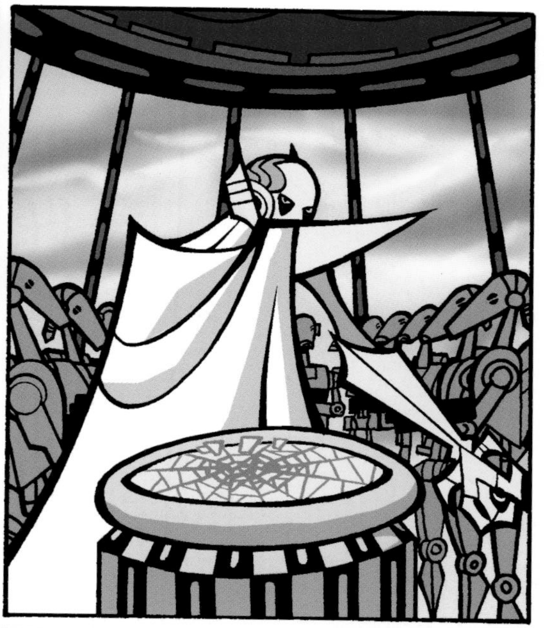
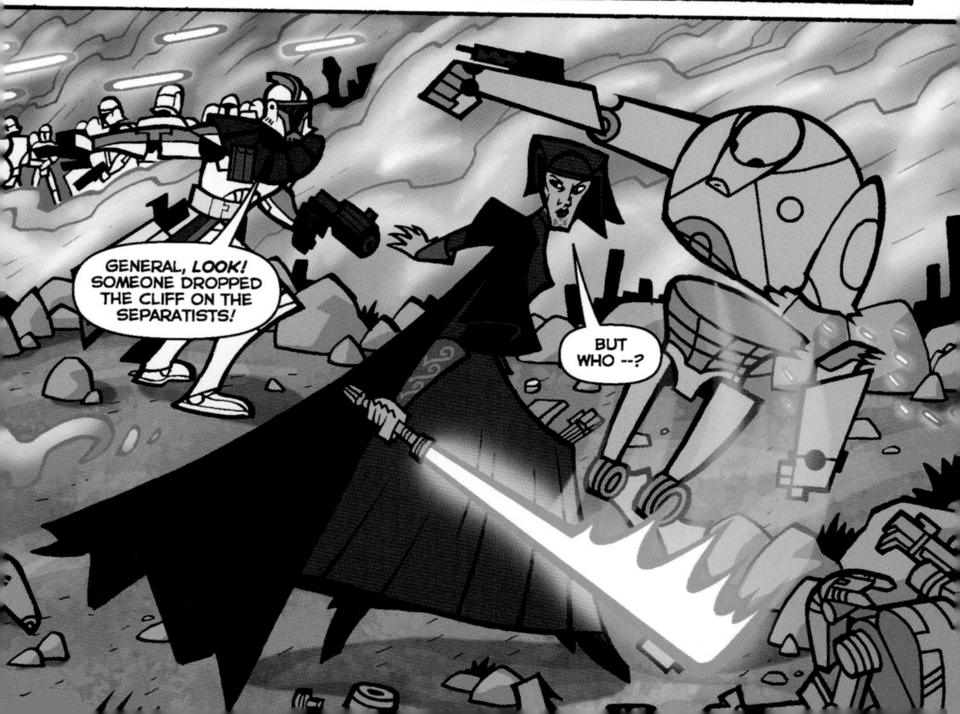
GENERAL, *LOOK!* SOMEONE DROPPED THE CLIFF ON THE SEPARATISTS!
BUT WHO --?

THE END

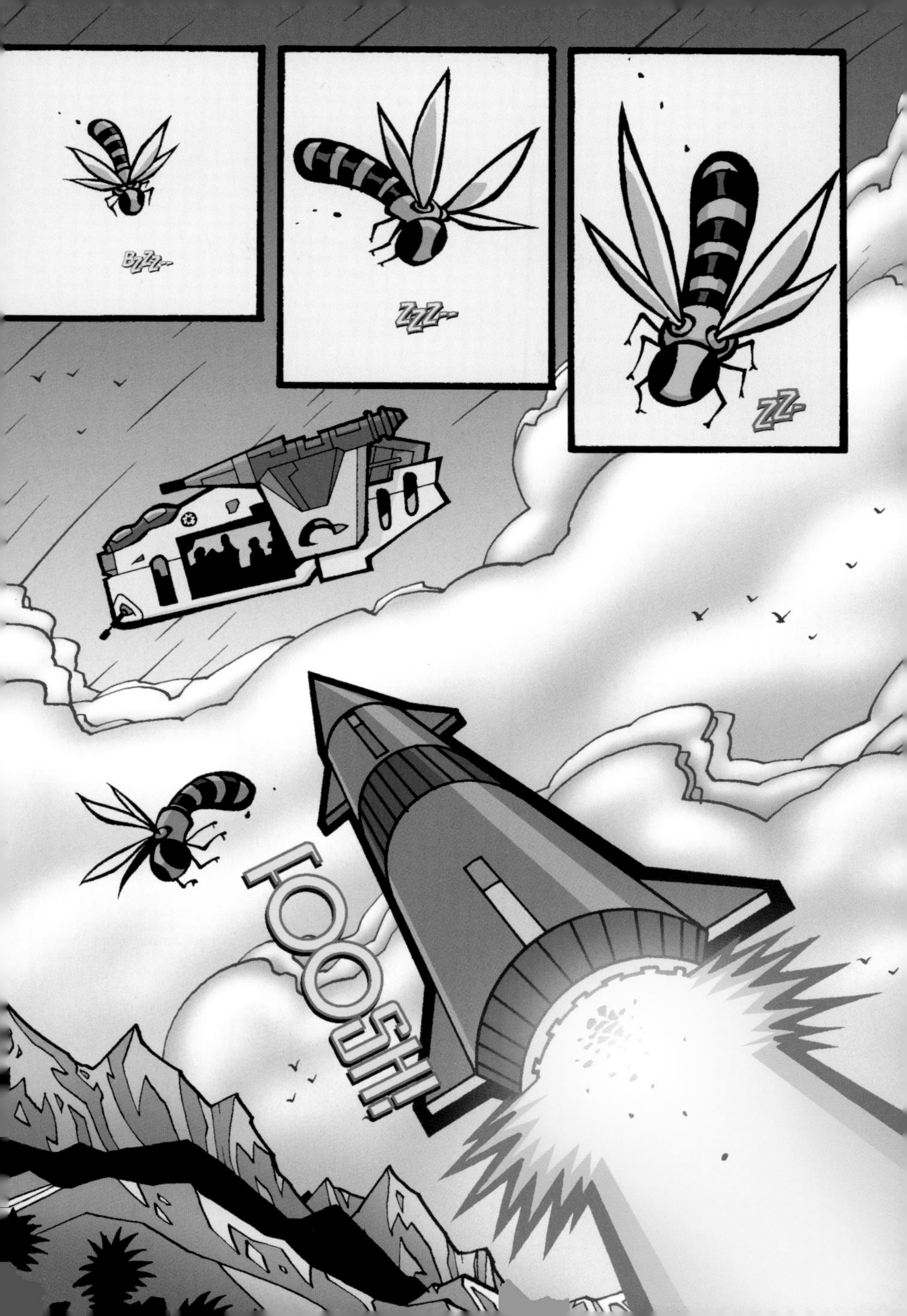
BZZZ--
ZZZ--
ZZ-
FOOOSH!!

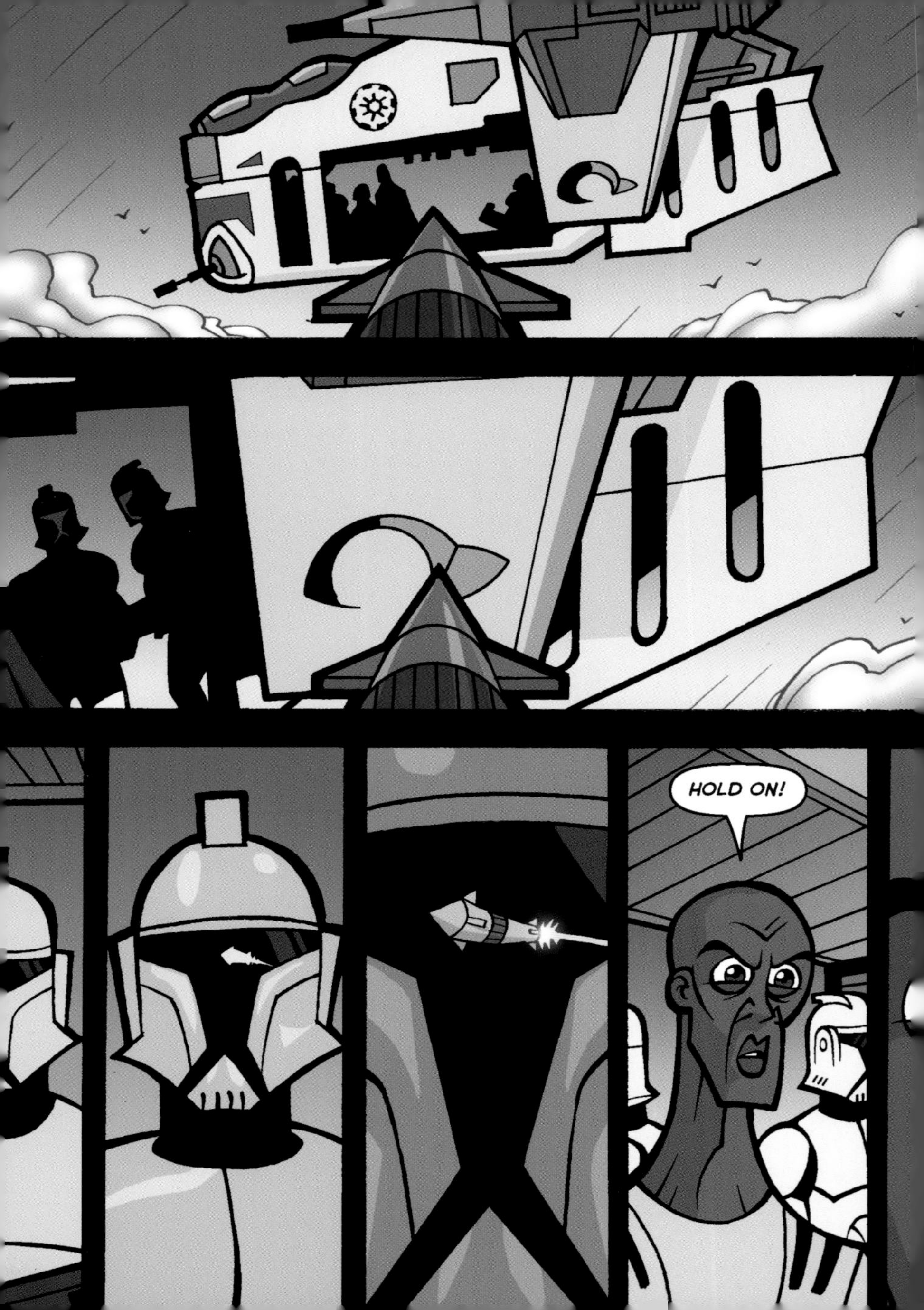
HOLD ON!

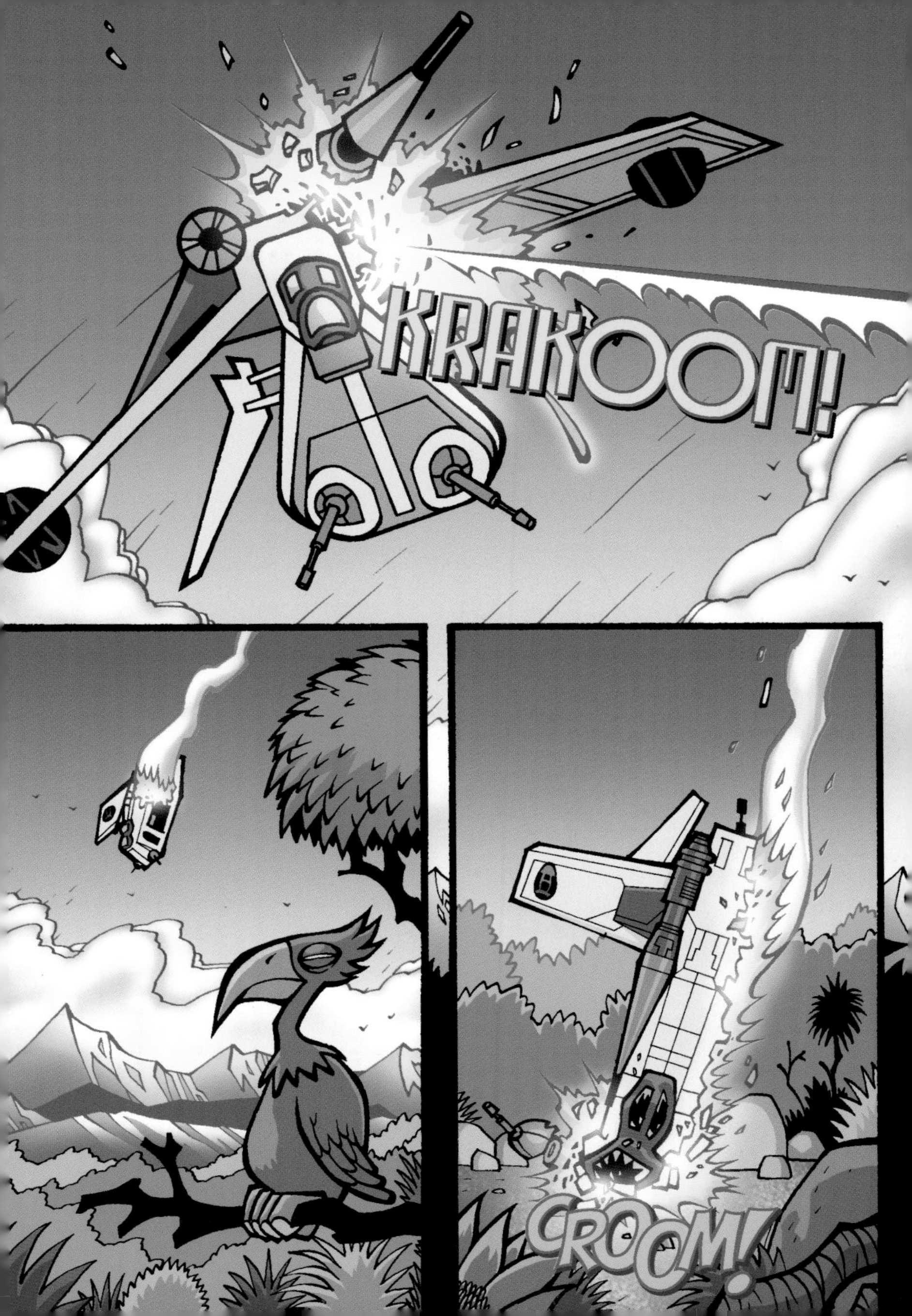
KRAKOOM!
CROOM!

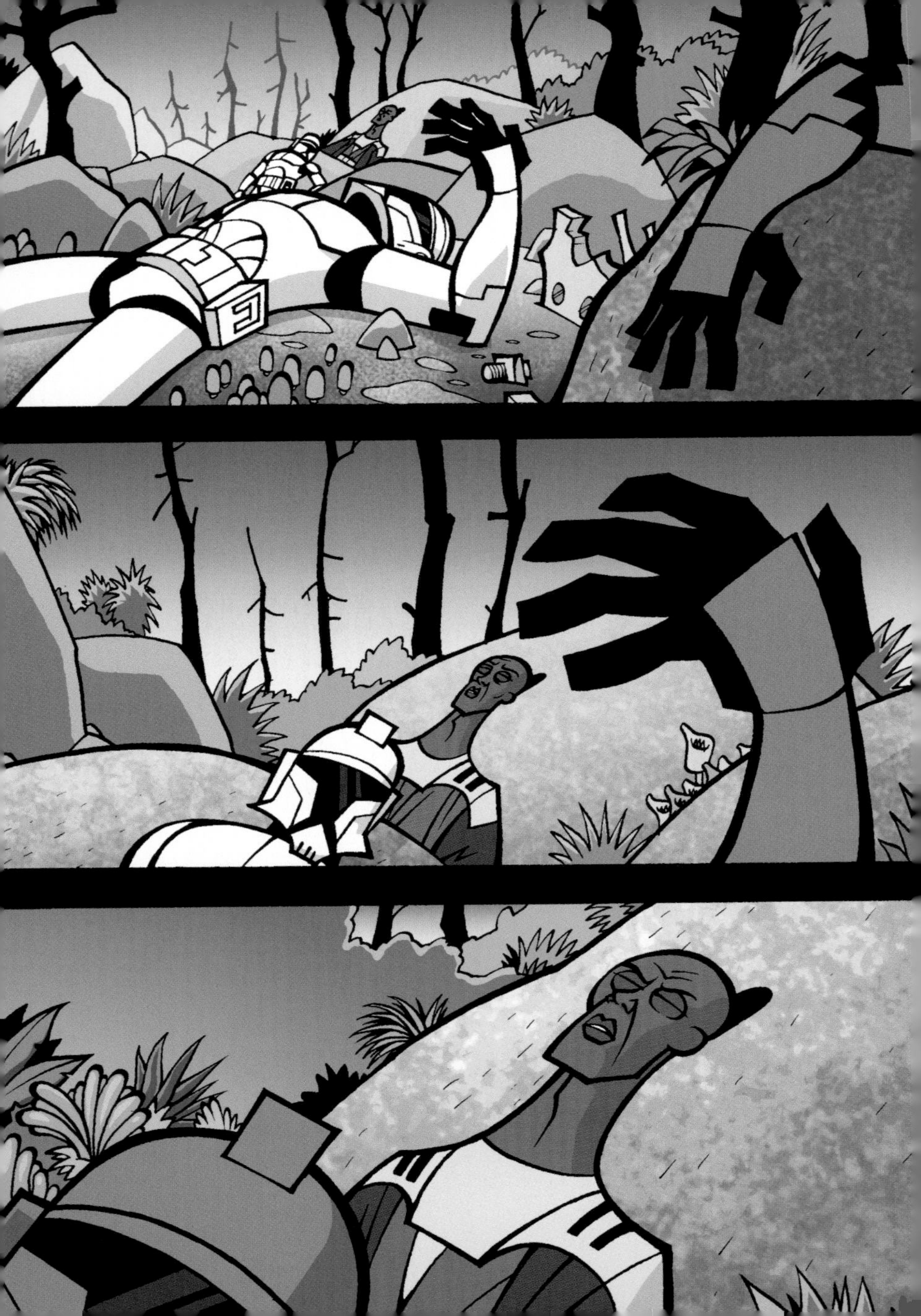

WEAK...

BUT I MUST MOVE...

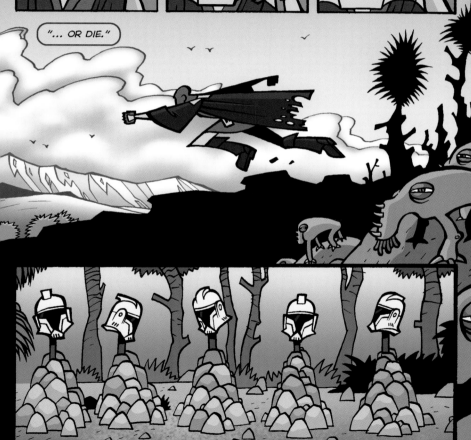

"... OR DIE."

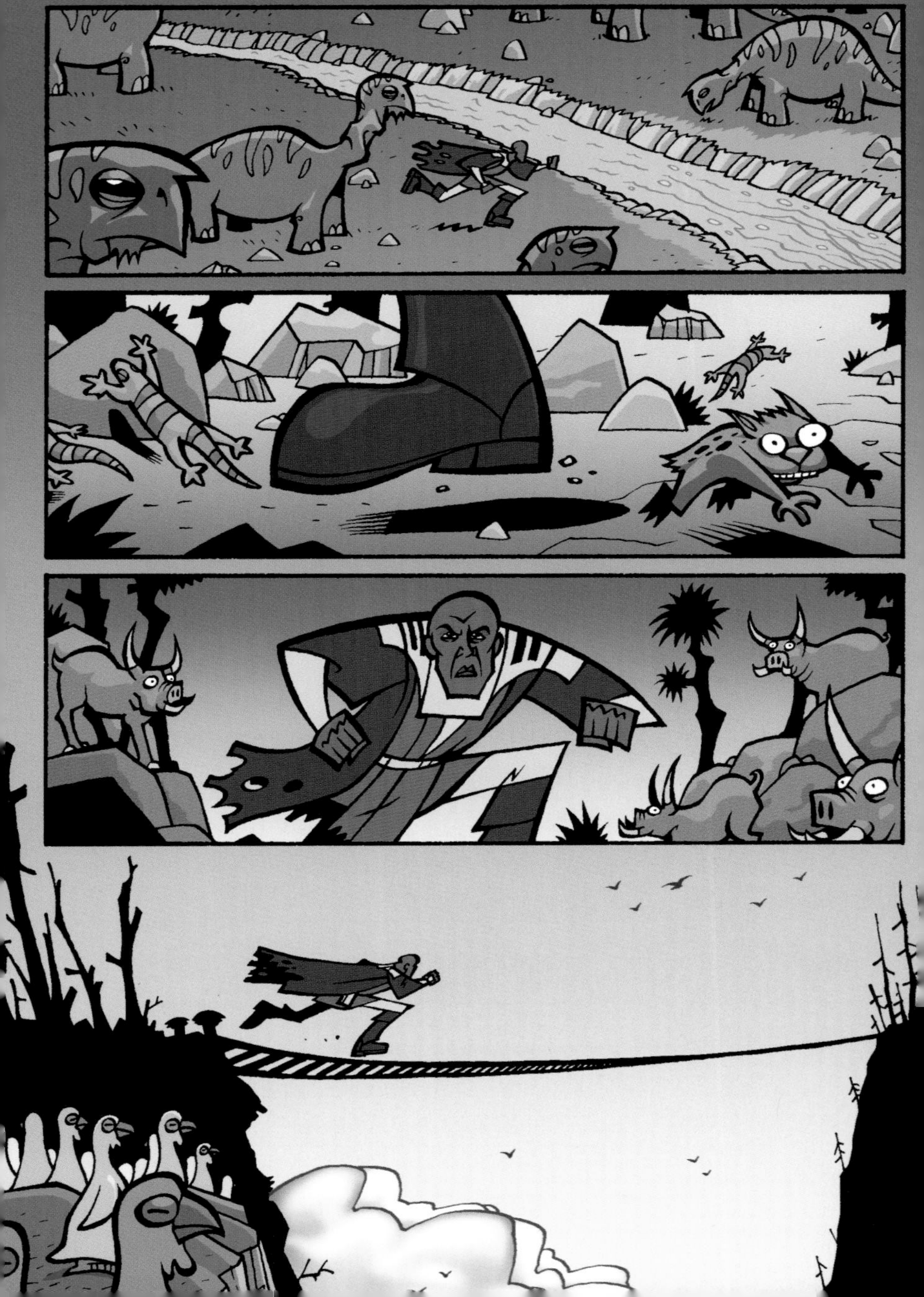

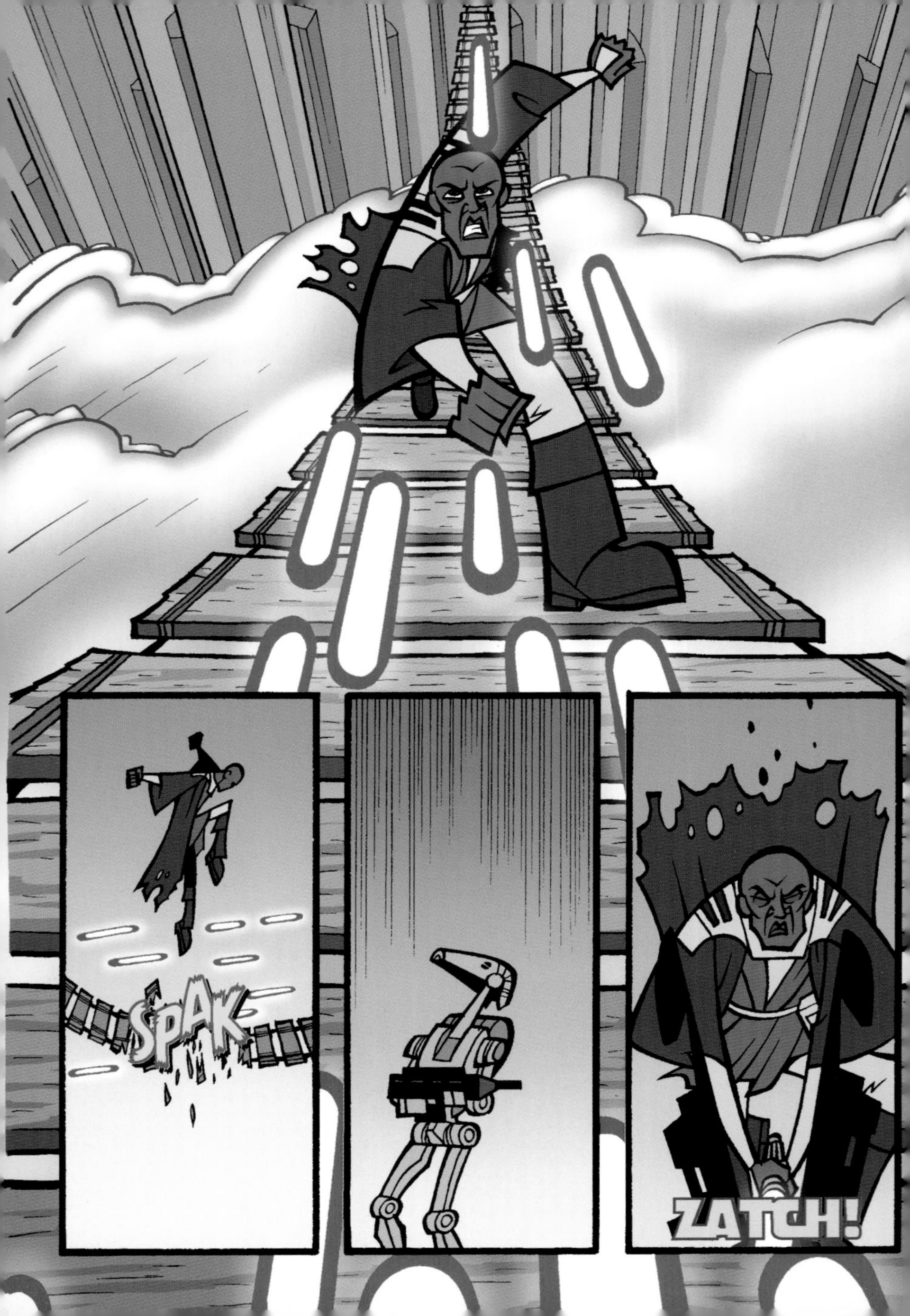
SPAK
ZATCH!

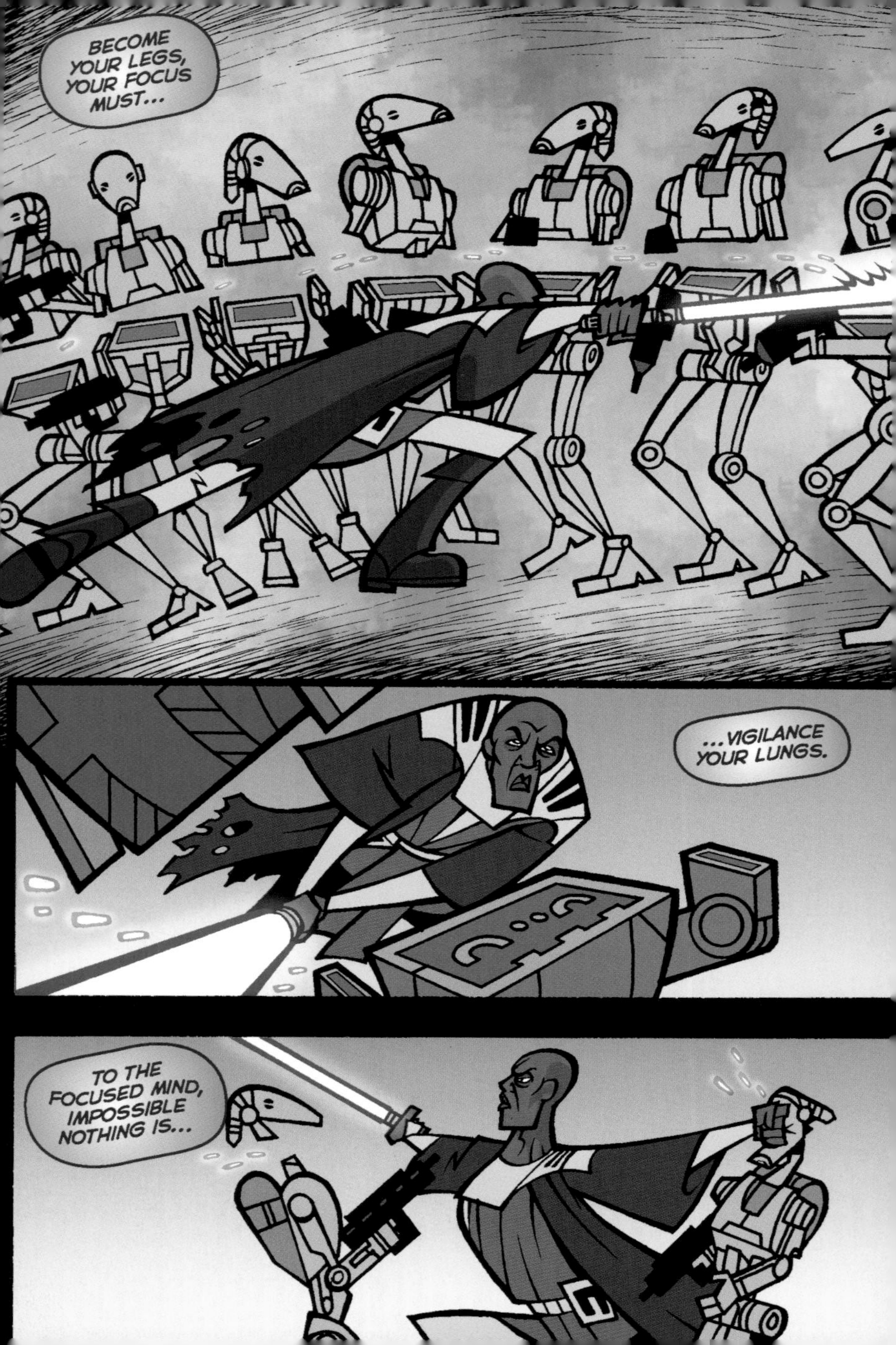
BECOME YOUR LEGS, YOUR FOCUS MUST...
...VIGILANCE YOUR LUNGS.
TO THE FOCUSED MIND, IMPOSSIBLE NOTHING IS...

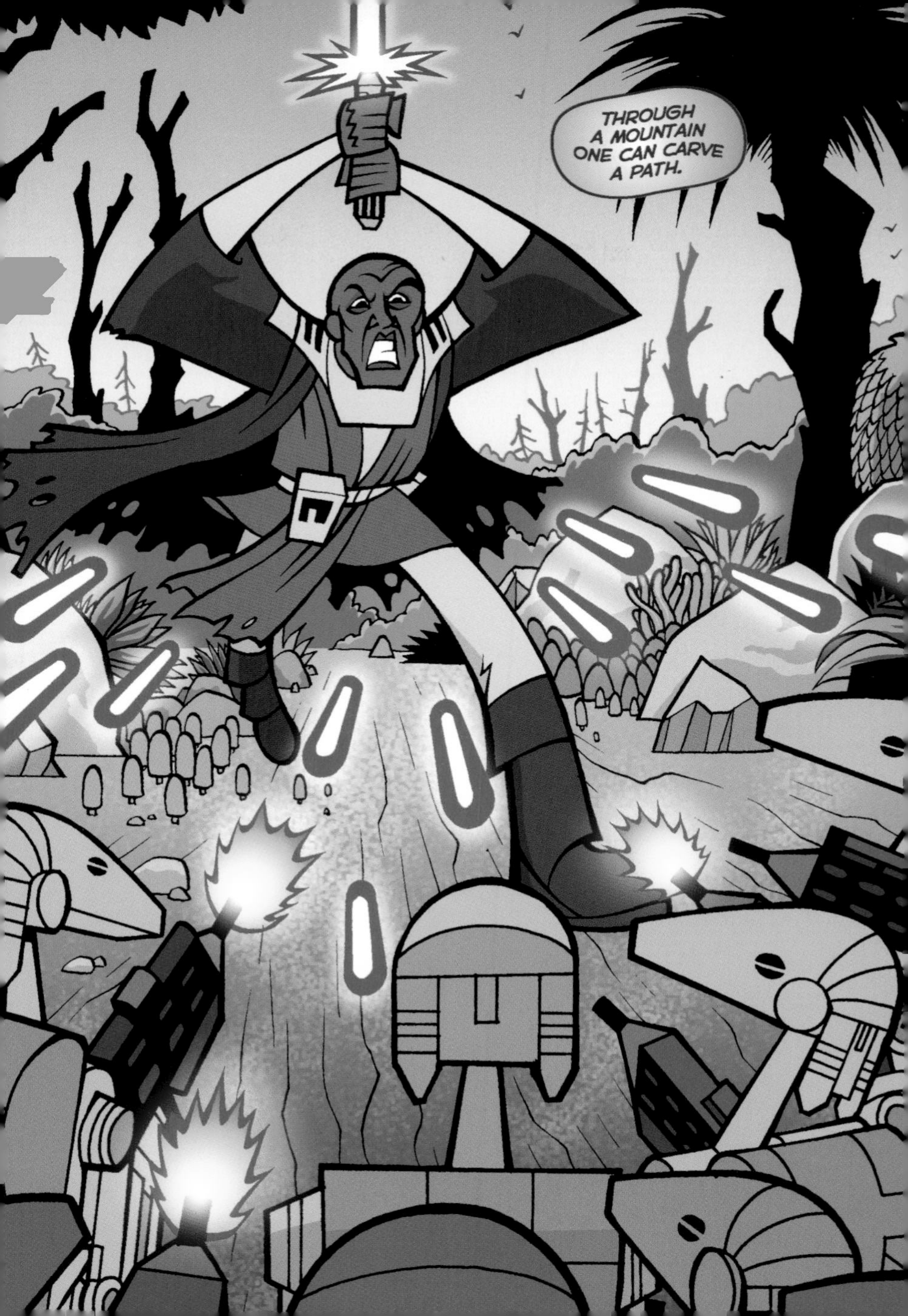
THROUGH A MOUNTAIN ONE CAN CARVE A PATH.

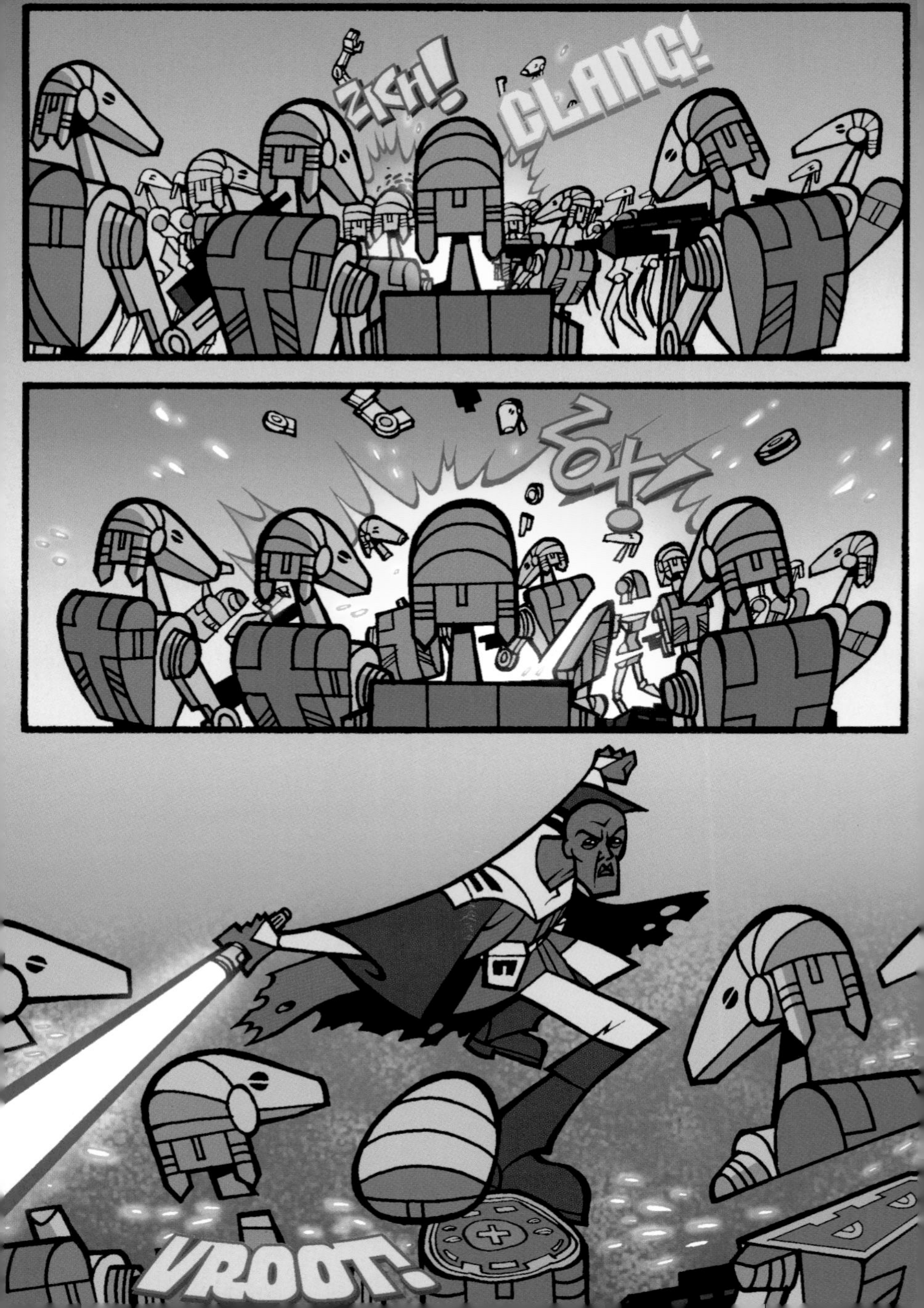
ZICH!
CLANG!
ZOK!
VROOT!

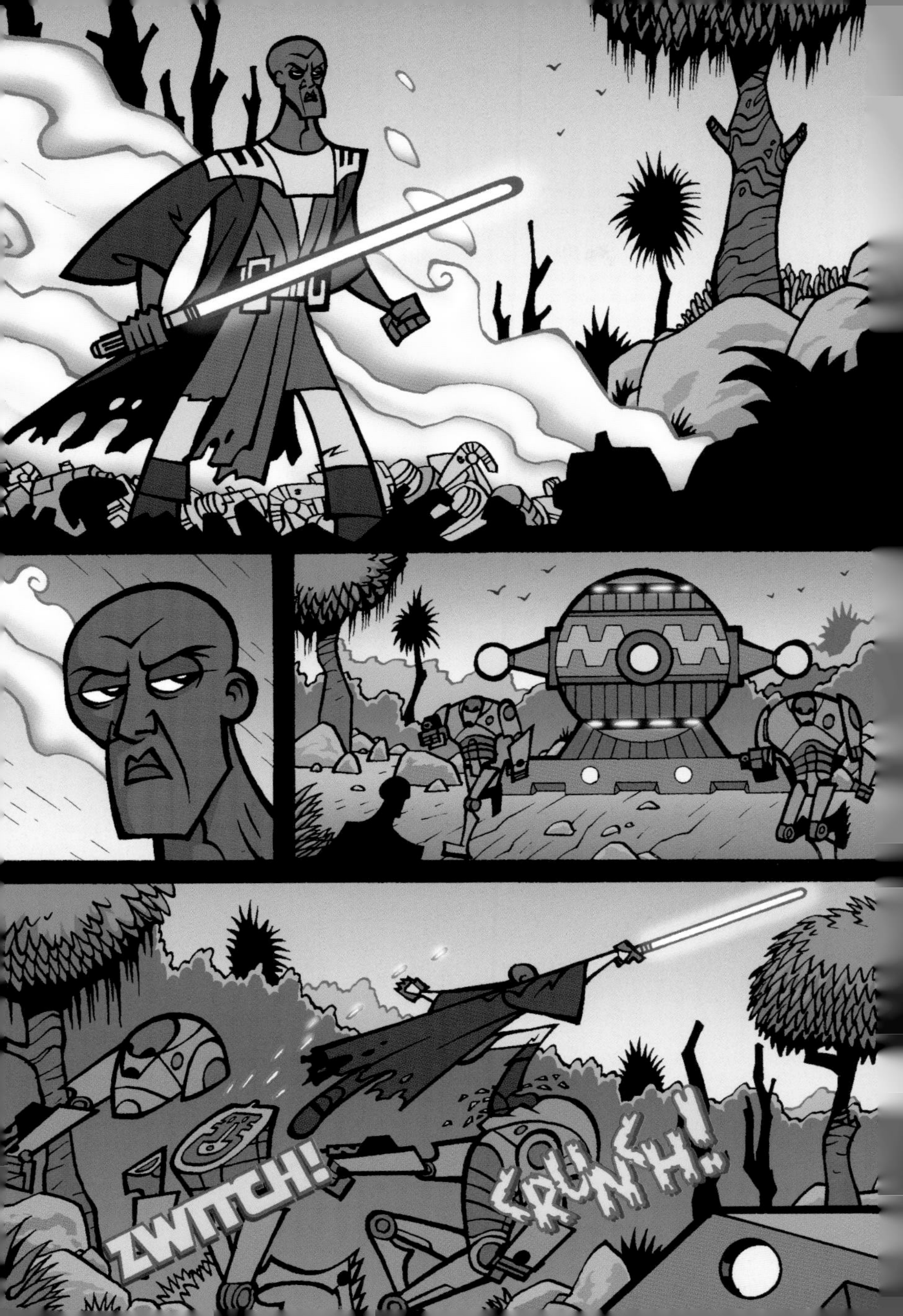
ZWITCH!
CRUNCH!

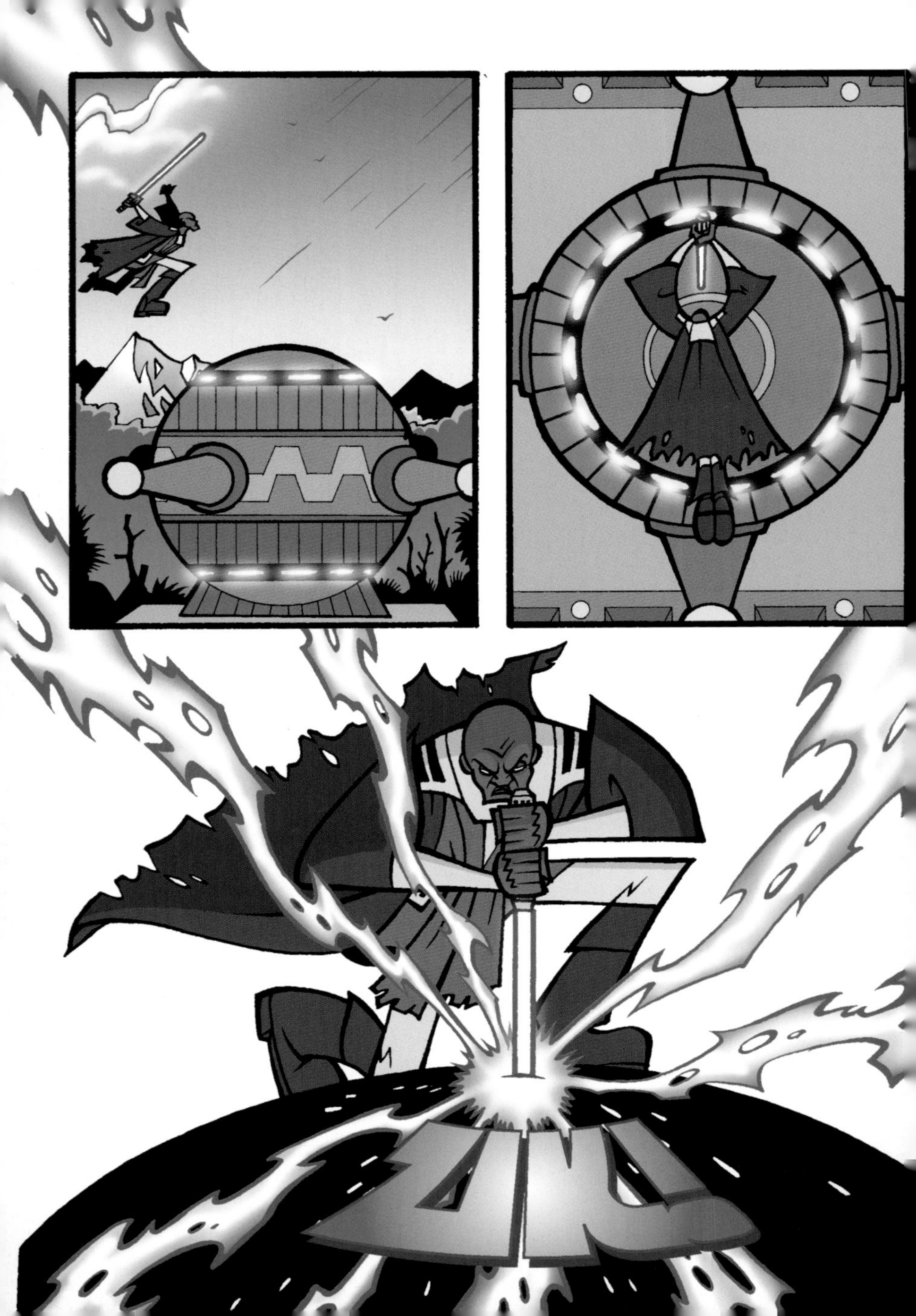

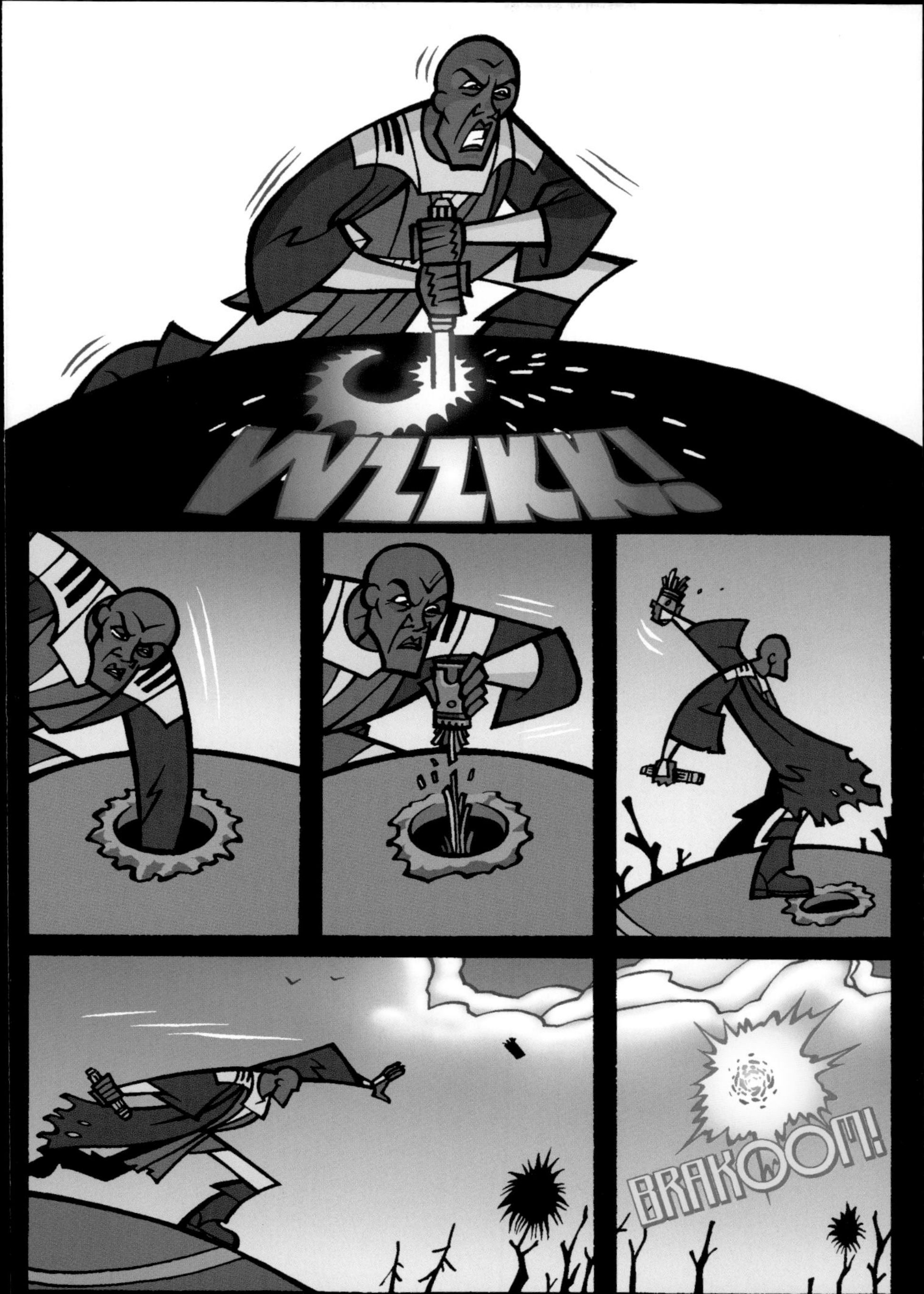
WZZKK!
BRAKOOM!